Writing Fanta

The Top 100 Best Strategies For Writing Fantasy Stories

By Blaine Hart
Copyright © 2015

Check Out all My Books and Audio Books
at: www.LordHartRules.com

Table of Contents

Introduction

I want to thank you and congratulate you for downloading the book, "Writing Fantasy: The Top 100 Best Strategies for Writing Fantasy Stories."

Fantasy is a classic component of fiction, described as a genre that typically includes imagined beings, the use of magic or superpowers, otherworldly settings or supernatural phenomena. You can also find animals–whether sentient or beastly, original or mythical–in fantasy books along with human-like individuals from multiple races (e.g., goblins, ogres, giants, elves). Classical fantasy tales are often set during medieval times, while others, bordering on science fiction, take place on different planets in imagined time structures. While I have just described fantasy writing for you in a few short sentences, it is a much broader genre than can be adequately represented by a brief definition. Although some fantasy may appear quite limited, many writers view it as an opportunity to exercise their creativity and experiment with novel characters, imaginative settings, and highly original stories. In many ways, the genre of fantasy is limitless.

While fantasy has its roots in ancient mythology and folk tales orally handed down the generations, its modern form was established and strongly influenced by a fairly obscure Scottish former minister named George MacDonald. MacDonald's first work, *Phantastes,* established a blurring of the "real" world by creating an alternate reality that overlaid it. He then peopled it with characters alive and of the afterlife, and melded timeless wisdom seamlessly into its pages.

You may not know George MacDonald by name, but you have experienced the results of his innovation. MacDonald is the primary influence of such fantasy authors as J. R. R. Tolkien, Lewis Carroll, and C. S. Lewis. The latter was once heard to remark, "I have never written a book in which I did not quote from him."

One element that separates fantasy from any other genre is the **Suspension of Disbelief.** This term, coined by poet and philosopher Samuel Taylor Coleridge, speaks to the reader's willingness to believe something unrealistic in exchange for entertainment. For example, everybody knows that elves don't live underneath your living room floor, but many are willing to let go of that fact while reading a story about it. The suspension of disbelief enables writers who have a vast, active imagination to become fantasy writers by freeing them from some of the restrictions of mundane life.

There is no better way to engage your imagination than by writing fantasy, where virtually every detail of the story may be designed by you. You can tell an amazing tale with few limits, while delighting your audience. If you often find yourself dreaming up different worlds, different races, or plenty of action, then fantasy writing might just be for you.

Writing a fantasy story can be a great deal of fun and enjoyment but it also has a few requirements. Since fantasy is a highly complex genre, writing fantasy can be compelling, exciting, and, of course, challenging. In addition to knowing how to encourage the suspension of disbelief in your readers, a fantasy writer must also have the skills required of all authors, knowing how to write a solid plot and develop engaging conflict. Fantasy differs from other genres in that most stories feature a unique world that the writers often build themselves. Creating a whole new world requires more time and dedication than a non-fantasy tale. Since there are so many unknowns, writers often find themselves spending much time describing and explaining background material. This created material can become quite extensive. Some writers go so far as to choose to create new languages, races, species, weapons, or even physical laws within their story world. This too will also take extra time and concentration, first to design, and then to present to the reader. Fantasy writing requires more creativity and a higher degree of open-mindedness from its writers than other genres. You will likely find it necessary to to come up with original words and terminology to describe geography, weapons, magic, classes of people or animals, and anything else relevant to your fantasy world.

This book contains proven steps and strategies to help you write a successful, well-structured, and exciting fantasy story. You will discover the preparatory steps unique to writing fantasy, as well as general fiction writing tips to help set yourself up for success. You will also discover how to create the basics of a fantasy story, including building an original story world, picking your subgenre, deciding on a theme and a story goal. Since fantasy writing requires in-depth, complex characters, there is a whole chapter in this book dedicated to developing characters just for fantasy, including everything from archetypes to naming. Finally, you will discover how to write an amazing ending for your fantasy story, one that will leave your readers dying to read more!

Chapter 1: Get Ready for Fantasy

So you've got a wonderful idea and you're feeling inspired to finally start writing your fantasy book. You sit down at your computer, open up a blank document and just start typing away as fast as you can, right? Think again. While many people imagine it is plausible to do just that, there is actually one very important step you should take if you want to be successful at any type of writing, not just fantasy. That step is **preparation**. Authors prepare themselves to write their next best-seller no differently than athletes prepare to win a game. Preparation helps you anticipate each part of your story and frees your creativity to develop entrancing ideas. Proper preparation will help reduce any anxiety you may have about your writing venture.

As an author, I believe preparation is the most vital part of writing a book. I also believe that everybody has their own personal way of preparing. Writing is a creative activity in itself. I know several authors who each have their own unique preparation routines. It all depends on you and your personal preferences. In this chapter, I will discuss some of the best ways to prepare yourself for the task of fantasy writing, but it's up to you to pick out what suits you best. The first few tips will be about preparing to write in general, followed by some of the best ways to prepare specifically for writing fantasy.

So, exactly how *does* one prepare to write an impressive fantasy novel?

The Meaning of Success

How do you define a successful writer? There are probably as many definitions as there are writers. Many would argue that a successful writer has a special talent or skill. Others would define a successful writer as one who has obtained special training or reached a certain level of notoriety. A successful writer may also be someone with connections in the publishing industry.

Here is my personal definition: I believe a successful writer is a person with a talent for writing, who is also willing to devote time to perfecting their craft. The craft can be perfected through trial and error, by taking classes, or through self-education (by reading books like this one, for example). A successful writer is a person who can learn from the critiques of others and push himself to grow as a writer. A successful writer writes regularly, even when it's not relative to his or her current work. A successful writer writes and rewrites, edits and re-edits. A successful writer is passionate about getting across a message.

Of course, it helps to network with and meet different publishers. You can start building those relationships by attending writing events and seminars, all of which can help you improve your craft.

You may think a successful writer is one who ultimately gets published and makes enough money to retire at a young age. Although that level of success can be extremely difficult to achieve, it is not impossible. Most people know that J.K. Rowling, author of the Harry Potter series, started out as a struggling single mom. Today she is the well-known author of multiple books, many of which have since been turned into highly popular movies. When it comes to publishing, especially fantasy novels, it is super important to **never give up!** Unless you are thinking about self-publishing, keep this in mind: Many famous fantasy books were rejected numerous times by major publishers, including the first *Harry Potter* book, *A Wrinkle in Time, The War of the Worlds, The Wizard of Oz* and even *Twilight*! Look at how popular all of those books are today–because the authors never gave up, even when faced with multiple rejections and frequent criticism.

While connections in the writing world can definitely help you get ahead, it is essential to know what publishers and readers are looking for. There is nothing wrong with contacting publishers directly, to learn what they are interested in publishing. Check out bestseller lists and look for common subjects and themes. Monitor news outlets and keep abreast of trending topics of interest. All of these can help you frame your story as an audience magnet. While fantasy stories often attract a very specific audience, you can still use any type of theme or topic within your story to give it a unique creative twist. For example, at the time of this writing, police brutality is a widely discussed topic in the United States, with people either in favor of the police or against the police. If you wanted to integrate this into a fantasy story, you could apply it to the authority figures in your book. Let's say there is a group of vigilante swordsmen in your story who take crime into their own hands. One way to create conflict would be to have the townspeople be in favor of, or in opposition to the group, then give each side a reason to take that stance. For example, those against the group may not agree with the violent measures they take, while those promoting the group are happy because crime is going down.

Maybe you are not interesting in being published. If you just want to write for yourself, you are still a writer; your definition of success is just narrowed down to an audience of one.

I highly recommend taking some time to write down your definition of success. Writing about it will help make it solid in your mind as you continue your literary quest.

Define Your Writing Goal

Once you have defined what it takes to be a successful writer, you should define your writing goal. If you've read any of my other books, then you know how much of an emphasis I place on setting goals, when it comes to being successful at anything. Setting goals as a writer is a little more complex than setting goals for dieting or fitness. Why? As a writer, you actually have *two* goals: your own personal goal and the goal of providing your audience with a satisfying experience.

Your personal writing goal is a variable. You might set a long-term goal to write a novel, a short story, or a series of stories. Your long-term goal could even be to become a published author. Your short-term goals should provide stepping-stones to your long-term goals and help you, slowly but surely, achieve ultimate success. For example, if you want to become a published author, then your short-term goals should include writing your first novel. However, to write your first novel, you will need an additional set of even shorter-term goals that include the completion of each chapter. To achieve those goals, you will probably need to set daily writing objectives. Many authors set a specific word count quota in order to help them stay on track and finish within a desired timeframe.

No matter what your writing goal may be, it is important to remember your ultimate objective. Every author must work toward this goal to be successful (by their definition). Part of that success means you must know how to gain popularity with your target audience; you must provide your readers with an **emotional experience.** To achieve this, you must first recognize why people want to pick up a book in the first place.

Most people who enjoy reading say they see it as an escape from their own reality. Many readers like to put themselves in a different world, so they can experience emotions they otherwise wouldn't encounter in everyday life. Readers like to feel moved, touched and inspired. They like to feel danger, fear, and suspense. They like their hearts stirred up to feel relief, happiness, and sadness. You can achieve each of these emotions through the writing of fantasy.

This is why it is so important to learn multiple techniques and elements of fantasy writing. If your book is boring and the pace drags, your readers will not be able to immerse themselves in the story and will more than likely put your book down after the first few pages. If your book is filled with conflict and emotion, your readers will get what they're looking for, especially if you provide periodic release from the tension and at least temporary resolution to high emotions. You will learn more about how to successfully provide your readers with an emotional experience as we progress through this book.

Before we go further, take out a piece of paper or grab your journal and jot down the following writing goals. Your **personal** goal can be vague at this point because it will become more clearly defined as you continue to write onwards in your life. For your **audience** goal, you can simply state that you will provide your readers with an emotional experience, returning to make with more specific information as your story's purpose becomes more fully defined.

Figure out What Writing Level You Are On

The next step is to figure out what level you are on as a writer. I say this because it writing is a process of continuous personal growth and professional skill. You must know where your current skills lie, compared with where you want to be. When figuring out what level you are on, you must be completely honest with yourself, otherwise you will never have a reason to improve. Writing skill is generally marked by four levels. You start off as a novice, then progress to the inexperienced writer stage, followed by the experienced writer stage, until you rise to the top as an expert writer.

A **novice** writer is typically just starting out. That's okay–everybody has to start somewhere. A novice writer usually knows that he or she wants to write something and has the ambition to get themselves started, but they may not understand what is necessary to really pack a punch with an audience or how to actually put a book together. An **inexperienced** writer is typically someone who has exercised their writing talent before and may know how to put a book together, but they still need to improve their skills and sharpen their craft. An **experienced** writer is dedicated to writing and probably attends classes, seminars and networking events. This writer may have even self-published a few times. An **expert** writer is one who has written several works and is familiar with both the craft and the ins and outs of publishing. She has connections among other writers and publishers, and may even have been published by a major publishing house.

Ask yourself where you think you stand on the writing spectrum and make a note of it. Part of your writing goal can be to move up a level until you've reached the status of an expert. Always remember that no matter what level you're on, there is always room for improvement; writing is a lifelong growth process.

Get Organized

As a writer, organizing should be at the top of your priority list for two reasons. First, your workspace must be easy to navigate; you must know where to find things without wasting precious writing time hunting around for them. Secondly, people tend to work most efficiently and creatively in an uncluttered environment. A clean and neat working area can actually make you feel good about yourself, which only feeds productivity and creativity. I'm reminded of a friend who was visited in his office by a well-dressed and neatly coiffed woman. The lady took one look at his desk, piled high with papers and research books, sniffed slightly, and stated, "You know; a cluttered desk is a sign of a cluttered mind." My friend thought for a moment, then looked up at the woman, and asked, "Then, what does an empty desk signify?"

Personally, I'm way too distracted by a mess; any type of clutter pulls my focus away from my work. Consequently, here are my personal workspace organizational tips:

- Keep a towel or duster nearby and dust your work area once a day. This helps keep your workspace clean and avoids upsetting your allergies, if you have any.

- Keep wires (such as your laptop charger, printer cord, and associated USB cables) together and organized, using twist ties.

- Put your pens, pencils, and scissors together in a pen holder.

- Keep your important papers together in a paper tray or a file rack.

- Avoid eating or drinking in your workspace, but if you do, clean up the area immediately afterwards.

Assuming that you're using a computer to write your book, it is also important to stay digitally organized. I know from personal experience that when you start to write a book on your computer, one document can quickly turn into many. I often use individual documents to track characters, chapter notes, a timeline of events, synopses, and outlines. It is easy to lose track of those files within your hard drive, especially if you have a lot of stuff on your system.

I have recently discovered that Microsoft OneNote can take care of all my digital organization concerns. This software acts as a digital notebook and allows you to keep all of your information in one place, yet order it in any number of different ways. If you have handwritten notes in a physical notebook, you can import them into the program, and in that way keep everything together and easily accessible. OneNote is available through Microsoft. If you're going to do a lot of writing, it's seriously worth downloading. OneNote has saved me a ton of time and energy!

If you aren't using a program like OneNote, my next best suggestion is to keep all your story resources in a single computer folder. For example, to organize your current writing project, you could create a folder on your desktop, name it after your story, and save everything in that single location. If your folder holds more than ten items, I suggest you manage them by creating subfolders within the master story folder. Order these folders according to what makes sense to you. You may wish to put all your preparatory information in one folder, with your draft text in another. You may wish to keep each chapter's text and related research documentation in a separate folder. You may feel the need to organize your work in any of a number of ways. The key is to organize your work in a way that is fairly unambiguous and makes sense to you; after all, you want to be able to put your finger on each part of your project at a moment's notice.

Although you may not immediately identify these next items as aspects of writing, you do need to organize your time, your energy, and your money. If you are working under a deadline, you automatically understand the importance of managing your time. Even if you are not required to meet an externally imposed deadline, I recommend setting a rough target date for completion of your next writing project, then scheduling your work to meet that objective.

Parkinson's Law states that work expands to fill the amount of time allotted to it. If you don't set a deadline, guess what? Your writing project may well take until doomsday to complete! You will work a lot more efficiently if you divide the work up into manageable chunks, then shoot to complete each chunk in a reasonable amount of time.

Giving yourself a "due date" will stimulate you to write on a regular basis. Writing a book does take time, but if you manage it appropriately, it's not as bad as it may seem. You can manage your time several ways, but the most popular time management technique for writing is to set a daily writing quota for yourself, in terms of number of words. There are two possible ways to set both a writing quota and a deadline. The first way is to decide how much you want to write each day and divide the total size of your book, in number of words, by the by that amount. This will give you the number of days it will take to complete your first draft. You can map this on a calendar to determine your projected completion date. The other method is to decide when you want to finish your first draft, and then work backwards from that date, calculating how many writing days you have before the deadline. Divide the total estimate for the book's word count by the number of days you plan to work, and you will know how many words you will need to write each day in order to meet your deadline.

Managing your time also includes planning breaks. Our bodies were not designed to sit still for hours on end. Recent studies have shown that as little as three hours of inactivity can be enough to affect our bodies negatively. Eyestrain is also possible in this line of work. It is important to take the eyes off the computer at least a couple times an hour, to look around you. When you can, take a few minutes outside; your eyes need to relax by looking into the distance for a change, and your whole being will benefit from a little intake of fresh air and natural sunlight.

We also need to periodically give our minds a break from thinking about the current writing project. Unfortunately, the mind does not have an "off" switch; the best way to give your mind a break is to divert it with something else that requires your attention. Any physical activity that requires a little attention will serve as a healthy break for both mind and body. I sometimes go outside to play with the dog or pull weeds in the garden. If I can't get outside, even a little light housecleaning is enough to get me moving and distracted from the computer for a few minutes.

The final organizational issue involves managing your money. You may not think about your writing costing money, and for the most part, you are correct. But you will likely incur a few expenses, if only for printer paper and ink for occasional printouts, the cost of internet access, for conducting research, and for communication with potential publishers. In addition, you may choose to invest in books that will help you as a writer; you may enroll in personal improvement classes, or pay for professional editing. Many writing seminars and conventions also cost money to attend. It is wise to allocate at least a small amount in your budget for writing expenses.

Pick a Writing Space

Every author needs a writing space – the place where you do the majority of your work. The most popular spots are at a desk in your home (preferably in a home office) or at a coffee shop, library, or another public venue. Some people can't focus when working in a public place like a coffee shop, but others thrive there. I've tried working on my laptop outside on several occasions but I've found it difficult when I don't have shelter from the sun. My personal preference is to sit at my desk and work. You might find it practical to work from your couch. Whatever you choose, set up your space in a comfortable location where you can work most productively. One friend, who was actually writing a fantasy story about an apocalypse, viewed through the eyes of birds, used to go to the local reservoir, sit on a bench and handwrite her story in a spiral notebook. Since the story was set in a reservoir, she found it most inspiring to actually write the story from a similar location. Although you can't physically step into a unique fantasy world you've created, I would highly recommend doing anything you can to approximate it within your workspace.

Eliminate Distractions

As a writer, I must admit my top excuse for slacking off is any of the multiple distractions that come my way. Working on a computer can be the worst, because email, social media, music, and other attractive activities are all too accessible. Even if you manage to avoid computer-based distractions, you can still access everything from your phone, which you probably keep close by. Then there are always the household distractions: your spouse, kids, or pets whose interruptions are almost irresistible. A quick and easy fix for this is to close the door to your office and hang up a "Do not Disturb" sign. That will probably work, as long as you allocate time and space elsewhere to interact with the people—and critters—in your life. I've tried writing outdoors before, but I've found it to be even more distracting than my children! I've endured everything from sunlight glaring on my screen and babies crying in the neighborhood, to visits from stray dogs.

As for digital distractions, I've found it helpful to work in full-screen mode. This way, my eyes are less likely to wander off to whatever lies behind what I'm writing. I've also made it a point to mute my phone until I'm done writing. For other audible distractions, I have discovered that earbuds will block out an incredible amount of noise, even without playing music through them.

Set the Mood

I personally find it helpful to set the mood before I begin a writing session. Depending on what kind of story I'm writing, I'll do different things. I've found that aromatherapy is a useful strategy for relaxing and getting into a positive state of mind. You can practice aromatherapy right in your own workspace by getting a small oil diffuser and some different oils to experiment with. My favorite way to fill a room with pleasant smelling aromas is with an <u>Aromatherapy Essential Oil Diffuser</u>. I've never liked the heat based delivery systems of other products, but this diffuser releases a fine mist of sweet smelling aromas and turns off automatically when it is finished. Some fragrant essential oils I recommend are:

- Lavender – known for its relaxing qualities, it also smells heavenly.

- Eucalyptus – a strong earthy, but pleasantly scented plant, thought to clear the mind.

- Marjoram leaves

- Peppermint

- Chamomile

- Cloves

- Cinnamon Bark

- Sage

- Rosemary

- Cardamom

- Verbena

In other situations, I find it helpful to play music in the background while I'm writing. The type of music I listen to usually depends on the genre I'm writing, but I try to stick to instrumental tracks; tracks with lyrics tend to distract me. If I'm writing a sad or depressing scene I like to listen to classical music, by composers such as Beethoven or Mendelssohn. If I'm writing a thrilling, action scene I'll go onto Spotify and look up soundtracks from my favorite movies to get me in the mood. If I can't really decide what to listen to, I'll just look up some Pandora instrumental tracks that are relaxing in general and let them play in the background. Fantasy Music for Writing by Lucas King is a really good track to start out with.

Practice Self-Discipline

Writing a fantasy book will take lots of self-discipline. I've written and published several books and have had people come up to me and say, "Wow, I could never do that!" I know from experience that writing is both challenging and grueling. I've gone through phases where I will barge right through a book and others where I'll start a book, only to drop it for a couple months. A disciplined life is essential if you hope to finish your book. For some people, self-discipline comes easily, but for those of you struggle to be disciplined, here are a few things you can do to reinforce your discipline choices:

1. Remind yourself of the consequences of *not* writing. A big self-discipline killer is when you say something along the lines of, "I'll do it when I feel like it." Well, what if you *don't* feel like it for the next couple of days? Let's say

you have made it a goal to write one chapter of your book each day, but one morning you wake up and just don't feel like writing at all. Even a day or two without keeping your commitment to yourself will set you back to the point that it will be difficult to completely catch up. It is much better to meet your goals, even if it hurts. You will feel much better afterwards.

2. Stop making excuses. When it comes to writing a book, there are no excuses. Writer's block is not an excuse either. When you say something like, "I'm too tired to write today" or "I can't think of anything to write," you're only setting yourself back. Give yourself a five minute activity break, then sit back down and get to writing. Write something every day, even if it's just a little bit of free-writing. Never let an excuse take over your chosen life.

3. Get yourself an accountability partner. Find somebody who will hold you responsible for accomplishing the things you have committed to. This can be a huge help. My suggestion is to find somebody who already serves as your mentor or role model; it will be harder to let down a person you respect and want to emulate than your best friend or your spouse. Sometimes best friends will let you off the hook far too easily. You want to find somebody who can be trusted to hold your feet to the fire when necessary.

Generate Self-Motivation

Along with self-discipline, you're going to need some self-motivation to get the job done. Procrastination is another obstacle that often prevents people from actually writing an entire book, so you'll need to know how to combat that before you even start.

One powerful technique many authors use as a motivator is to ask, "Why?" Why do you want to write? Popular answers include wanting to see your name on the cover or a desire to entertain people. Some people simply have a story that they need to get out. Go ahead and figure out your why. I encourage you to write this down and keep it visible in your workspace, to consistently motivate yourself to keep going.

Another motivational technique is to promise yourself a reward at the end. Writing a book is a big task, so if you have a big reward waiting for you afterwards, you're much more likely to finish. I can't define your reward –that's for you to choose–but make it something that you really, *really* want. You may choose a tangible object such as a new TV or a video game system; others choose a short vacation; but for some people, just seeing their book in print is reward enough.

Finally, I have found that physical exercise can be motivational as well. Exercising allows your body to feel alive, so you'll have an overall "feel-good" sensation to carry into your writing. I think that the better you feel physically, the better you'll be able to perform your writing. When I work out, I start to feel inspired to tackle other major accomplishments. Exercising is also a useful way to spend your "break" time. You already spend enough time sedentarily before your computer; break it up by moving your body, and you may be pleasantly surprised with some fresh ideas when you return to your writing.

Eat Before Writing

Don't forget to eat before you start writing! Eating a meal can give you a burst of mental energy, which you can then pour out into your book. If you try to write on an empty stomach, you may find it harder to concentrate; you might even do something crazy, like naming a character after food! The best types of foods to eat before writing are those that will stimulate your brain, such as:

1. Fruits and Vegetables – These foods are full of antioxidants that are good for fueling your creativity. Experts believe that blueberries are the most effective. Whip up some blueberry pancakes, a blueberry smoothie or simply snack on some blueberries straight up.

2. Omega-3 Fatty Acids – This substance is known to boost the functioning of your brain, which you're definitely going to need as a writer. You can provide your body with omega-3 fatty acids through fish such as salmon or mackerel, or through flax seed. If you don't want to eat actual fish, you can always supplement your healthy diet with fish oil capsules.

3. Milk – Drinking milk can help boost your memory because it contains a wonderful substance called choline. As a writer, your memory is important; after all, you want the details in your story to be consistent. You don't want Mary to have blonde hair on page three and then brown hair on page seven.

4. Glucose – Foods that contain fructose can help your concentration remain solid. Avoid the high fructose corn syrup or alternative sweeteners. Stick to healthier natural sugars such agave and stevia, or eat some fresh fruit.

5. Protein and Whole Grains – Protein and whole grains are essentials for keeping your body energized and healthy. Your best bet is to eat a big breakfast that contains these nutrients. For example, try chowing down on some whole grain toast and an egg.

6. Supplements – In some cases you can take supplements to help boost your energy and mental clarity. Supplements come in all types, such as fish oil, multi-vitamins, individual vitamins, and minerals such as calcium with magnesium. One of my favorite supplements for mental activity like writing is called Focus Formula.

Find Your Niche Audience

Before you start writing, you'll want to figure out exactly *for whom* you are writing. No book can ever appeal to every audience. Some books appear like they appeal to everyone, but that was not the case in the beginning. For example, people of all ages have read the *Harry Potter* series, but even those books originally started out as a series intended for school-age children. Yes, your book may eventually appeal to multiple audiences, but to become successful, it must first successfully reach a single audience. It is important to remember that different people like different things. Not everybody within your niche audience is going to like your book, but as long as you can make much of your niche audience happy, then you will have succeeded.

The first step in figuring out your niche audience is to determine what types of people your book may interest. Sometimes this requires being a little stereotypical. For example, the majority of chick lit readers are probably women, since those books focus on women's interests. Figuring out a niche audience for fantasy will require a little bit of guesswork and common sense, because there are no official demographics. From what I have picked up over the years, I would best guess that both genders enjoy fantasy, as well as all ages. Since fantasy has many subgenres, which you will discover in a few chapters, you may want to use those as a guide. For example, one subgenre of fantasy is historical fantasy. If I was researching a niche audience, I would try to find out the demographics on readers who enjoy historical fiction and narrow it down from there. If you're really having trouble figuring out your niche audience, you could turn to online writing forums or hang out in the fantasy section of a bookstore and interview the people you see there. You may gain important demographic information and even make a few friends in the process.

Another powerful tool for determining your niche audience is to figure out what **emotions** you want to instill within your readers. Sometimes your readers will fall in love with your main character, either because they want to be him or they want to know somebody like him. A geeky honor roll student might enjoy reading about heroic knights because he dreams of saving a girl and being a hero. The emotions found in fantasy often revolve around heroism, courage, friendship, honor and romance.

Once you have painted a picture of your audience, I recommend crafting an **Ideal Reader Profile.** Businesses often do this, so they can customize their products and services to meet the needs and expectations of their ideal customers. Having an Ideal Reader Profile on hand will enable you to easily write to appeal to those readers. In your profile, include relevant descriptives, such as religion, politics, education, gender, age, or favorite activities. This can also be helpful if you're planning to write multiple books targeted toward the same audience. Some authors stick to a style they've found successful and write multiple books directed toward the same group of people.

Write a Book You'd Like to Read

Let's face it—people read books for entertainment and escape purposes, so a boring book won't really do you any good. When you're preparing to write your book, plan to write something you would like to read. At least this will get you started on your way; it may even lead you to write a fantastic novel! I recall once reading an interview with Daniel Handler, the author of *A Series of Unfortunate Events*, in which he reported that his publisher asked him to write a book he would have liked to read as a child. That's how his entire series came into being. Approaching your book from this perspective will also allow you to explore your creativity. Don't be afraid to mix different elements and ask "what if" questions to come up with what seems like crazy storylines. If you think it would be interesting, it probably will be. You will discover more about this element later on.

Settle on a Length

Before you actually start writing your book, one thing you should do is decide how long your book will be. There actually is no "right answer." Your book can be as long as you want (or need). That being said, there are popular guidelines you can follow. If you plan on trying to get your book published, I strongly recommend calibrating your word count according to these genre guidelines:

- Fantasy – 110,000 to 115,000

- Young Adult – 55,000 to 70,000

- Children's – 20,000 to 55,000

- Picture books – 350 to 600

- Chapter books – 6,000 to 10,000

So if you wanted to write a standard fantasy book, shoot for the first figure. If you want to write one geared towards teenagers, use the young adult count as your guideline, and so on..

Here are also some general word count figures for the overall types of books:

- Short Story – 7,500

- Novelette – 7,500 to 17,500

- Novella – 17,500 to 40,000

Trying to write a fantasy book with a specific word count in mind can be challenging, especially if you're a first time writer. The real challenge lies in the fact that on one hand you don't want to compromise your story by leaving out critical details, but on the other hand, you don't want to overwhelm your story line with *too many* details. One possible strategy is to decide what type of book you're going to write (so you have a rough idea of how long it should be), then write with no restrictions. See how many words you end up with and then edit them down as necessary. This way you have your entire book written so you can better decide what to edit out and which parts to keep.

Create an Outline

Some writers prefer to create an **outline** before writing. Others are better off just opening a blank document and typing away, making up the story as they go along. Personally, I am an outliner. I think about my story in depth and tend to put the story line together before I actually start crafting it, but that's just my preference. Outlining helps me ensure that my story flows, another quality that is immensely important to holding the attention of your audience. I also like to write a synopsis beforehand so I know exactly where each twist and turn fits into the overall shape of my story. If you are better off writing on a whim, you might consider writing an outline *after* you have written most of the book. Writing an outline after the fact will help you check for balance and continuity in your writing.

Terrible First Drafts and Painful Criticism

No great book was ever written in one sitting on the first try. One writer friend says he usually goes through seven drafts before he is satisfied about sending his book to the publisher. Don't worry about achieving perfection on your first draft. I'm a perfectionist myself, so I know just how challenging a first draft can be. However, I also know that writing a story is a complex task that will require multiple phases for its completion. The beauty of writing is that you can go back as many times as you want and edit your story until it really *is* perfect.

Now, pretend you've just finished the first draft of your fantasy and you feel wonderful. You just know you have the world's next best-seller lying on your desk. You send your "baby" to your editor or have somebody you trust critique your text; it comes back to you with all sorts of markings, indicating multiple suggestions for change. This can be a serious blow to your ego. There's nothing more discouraging then to work hard at a creative task, only to have people find fault with it. However, remember this: yes, criticism hurts, but it's for the good of the book.

I remember the first story I published. I was so proud of it that I posted a couple chapters online to get readers' opinions. In retrospect, my first draft was absolutely terrible; I found out the hard way. After reading reams of solid criticism, I took another look at my tale and had to admit, "Actually, yeah this *is* pretty terrible." Only upon that admission was I able to go back and rework my story until I had something worth releasing to the world.

Mentally prepare yourself for what feels like destructive feedback about your work. Try to not take it *too* personally. Remind yourself that critiques are *not* meant to attack you as a person; after all, you requested the feedback in the first place! Secondly, those negative assessments of your work are a gift; they contain just what you need in order to improve your book until it has become the best story you can make it.

Read Other Fantasy Stories

One way to specifically prepare yourself for writing fantasy is to read other fantasy stories or do something else to immerse yourself in a fantasy world. For example you could play a fantasy-like video game such as Final Fantasy or Worlds of Warcraft. Just be careful not to steal any ideas. Instead, analyze how the characters in the story or game are developed in terms of personality, story goal, and dialogue. Also notice how the characters act and interact with one another. Finally, look at the elements of their world and take note of how each element is essential to the plot.

Research Myths and Legends

Try researching time-tested myths and legends to use as a basis for your story. Good starting points could include Celtic, Norse, or Medieval legends. Once you start researching myths and legends from one culture, it's easy to discover myths from other cultures. Keep your eyes peeled for legends about mythical creatures or lost civilizations and use anything you can use for inspiration. Again, be careful not to copy whole ideas that are not yours.

Look at Things Differently

Fantasy writing requires a good deal of imagination, often more than for any other genre. A good way to stir up your imagination is to learn how to look at things differently. This technique may require some practice to master but once you've got it down you may find yourself flooded with ideas. A good way to start is to take something simple from everyday life (such as a New York City street on a busy Monday morning) and look at it from multiple perspectives—that of a child, a teenager, a young adult, a middle aged adult, or a senior citizen.

Create Your World First

Before you start writing your actual story, it is important to create the world your characters will populate. This is important for several reasons. First, your world will have certain physical laws and cultural ways of life your characters will need to abide by. If you start writing your story without fleshing out these details in advance, you potentially create more work for yourself when it's time to edit for inconsistencies.

Secondly, creating your world before you write puts you in a position to know it better than anyone else. If you were to go on a guided tour, you would probably want your tour guide to know the land extremely well. After all, you are paying good money and expect the best possible experience. As the author, you are the tour guide for your readers. You want them to quickly feel at home in your story, so the better you know your world, the more effectively you can make it live for them. This is the basis for invoking suspension of disbelief, so you don't want to mess up this part.

Third, I think creating your world before anything else opens the door for inspiration. While you're busy actually creating the world, a really good idea for the story line might pop into your head that you can add to the plot. As your characters people your world, you may find they behave differently than you would otherwise imagine. Then you're well on your way to writing good fantasy.

Create Maps of Your World

You can also draw a map of your world, as part of your preparation. Some versions of J.R.R. Tolkien's books have maps of Middle Earth on the inside cover. This can help you visualize your world as you write; it can also help your readers envision the world they are entering. You don't have to be an artist to create a map; even a rough sketch will serve to guide you. However, if you really like the idea of including maps in your story, I would recommend using a website such as Fiverr to hire a graphic artist who can make a professional version of your maps for publication.

Plan Your Magic

If your story is going to contain magic elements, it is also a good idea to plan this out before you actually start writing your story. By planning your magic, you can create a master list of rules, limits, resources, and potential users. It is very important to clarify rules for using magic; otherwise your readers may think you're being lazy. In *Harry Potter*, for example, J.K. Rowling makes it a rule within her books that students are not allowed to use magic during summer break. Consequently, even before Harry does break out his magic that summer, massive tension has been created, adding conflict to the plot. If you are going to plan out magic, I would recommend making a master spreadsheet and listing each type of magic you include, along with its uses, limits, and needed resources. As you're writing the story, you can reference the master magic sheet to ensure that all of your details are consistent.

Eliminate Clichés

Unfortunately, clichés are not uncommon in fantasy writing. Some ideas and concepts have been recycled to the point that readers are craving something new and original. Be careful to avoid, or at least minimize your use of clichéd concepts, characters, and plotlines. It is expected that you will use fantasy creatures and imaginative story elements, but check to see whether the idea has been overdone before you claim it for your book. To check for clichés, survey the fantasy books on Amazon.com and see what other people are writing; then steer away from the most common ideas. Beyond that, here are a few fantasy clichés to avoid:

- A perfect hero, especially one chosen from obscurity to become a messiah figure

- Imagined cultures that are identical to already existing ones

- Stylized creatures (e.g., ogres, elves), without any changes or additions to their personality or abilities

- Anything simplistic, two-dimensional, be it a character, a political system or a plotline

- Imagined worlds that do not change, ever, across millennia

- Overused symbols, such as assigning white to the good character and black to the bad guy

Pick Which Details Are Most Important

Once you have created your world, chosen magic and figured out other details, pick out what is most important to convey to your readers. You don't need to show every single detail, just the ones that matter. Think of it as choosing the "right" details. For example, your world can be the most detailed world ever, but if it's not important for your readers to know the color of the sidewalks then don't focus on it.

Kickstart Your Creativity

In this final preparatory step, in order to start writing you will need to get your creativity going. Writer's block is often a writer's worst nightmare. Imagine getting everything ready, sitting down at your desk and then realizing that you don't have a clue what to do. However, it is important to write *something* every day, whether or not it's relevant to your story. Your body, mind, and spirit need the repetition. I highly recommend that you sit down to write at about the same time every day; after you have done this consistently, your body and your mind will accept the activity as a habit, and you will suffer less mental resistance to writing than if your schedule were haphazard.

One of the most popular ways to meet this requirement as well as motivate yourself to work on your main story is **freewriting**. Freewriting is when you sit down and write whatever comes into your head. For freewriting to work best, you should set a limit, such as three minutes or three hundred words. This way you won't get lost in time, neither will you wear yourself out. Challenge yourself to write straight through without going back to make changes. If you really want to challenge yourself, close your eyes and don't look at what you've written until your time is up.

Another effective creativity strategy is to randomly pick a handful of letters from the alphabet and use those letters to create a potential title for a book. Then go ahead and start writing its story. Your tale can be as short or as long as you want. This strategy can serve as a warm-up to your writing project, or it could even turn into a full-length novel if you like the idea well enough.

If you're feeling really unmotivated, you could use a few "story starters" or writing assignments as a warm-up prompt. Matthewdellar.com has some good fantasy writing prompts you can choose from to get started.

If you have already completed a book or a short story, a helpful creative writing strategy is to make up an alternate ending. Think about one of your favorite movies where they show another ending if you watch through the credits. If your story has a happy ending, perhaps you could write an ending that is slightly depressing. If your story has a sad ending, you might put a happy spin on it.

Alternatively, I sometimes find inspiration by reading one of my favorite authors' works, by watching a movie I've never seen before, or by entering into a new role-playing game. I think that when I explore new experiences I am reminded that the creative possibilities out there are endless. This alone will often fire me up to get started writing again.

Chapter 2: Dreaming up a Story

Once you have completed the necessary preparations, the next step is to figure out the basics of your fantasy story. **Story basics** are things that you need to ask yourself, such as "What type of fantasy book will this be?", "Where is the story set?", or "Where will the story begin?" Once you have these details worked out, then you can delve into the actual writing. In this chapter, you will discover how to strategically set up your book to be a best-seller by selecting your fantasy subgenre, choosing a setting, planning the action and other foundational items.

What is a Story?

A story forms when characters want what they can't have. Usually, this will generate in them some sort of **change**. Readers like to see your main character change and grow across the life of the story. The character's transformation should be realistic, because your readers will be experiencing it through his eyes. When a character comes to a new understanding in his life, views the world differently, or learns something about himself, a genuine shift will take place. This may occur near the end of your story, or it may build gradually, with the unfolding of your tale. As your main character experiences increasing discomfort–or a cataclysmic event–this sets up the **conflict** that is essential to any tale. Alternatively, the conflict may occur early and drive your character toward internal change. In this case, your character's inner conflict will push him into an internal confrontation at the **climax** of your story. As the main character undergoes change, this process will help shape your **plot**.

Why Write Fantasy?

Why write fantasy as opposed to any other genre? There are several reasons., the most popular being that fantasy provides an escape. When you're deep into a fantasy, you're not faced with your current relationship problems , the pressure of figuring out how you're going to pay the bills, or your need to decide what to do with your life. In fantasy, you are transported to a world where none of these exist. Secondly, fantasy helps remind people, especially adults, how important it is to use one's imagination. We easily get lost within the seriousness of the real world and forget the wonders of magic and creativity. Fantasy books help remind us to dream.

Fantasy tales can also serve as a type of therapy. Fantasy challenges readers to expand their perceptions and explore different ways to understand the real world. It can let you learn the consequences of certain actions as you vicariously experience them through your storybook hero. With some fantasy tales, you may absorb truths that your parents and teachers were unable communicate over years of trying.

Fantasy Genres

Genre is somewhat important to publishers and, ultimately, to your readers. It enables them to quickly identify your book, describe it to others, and list it appropriately online when you do get it published. It's easier to tell people, "This is a dark fantasy story," than to explain, "It's a book about a guy who is summoned to save the village from evil forces." Fantasy contains multiple subgenres, one of which may accurately fit the description of your story:

Contemporary/Urban Fantasy – These fantasy stories are set in modern times but contain fantasy elements.

Dark Fantasy – Fantasy stories that focus on dark elements, such as evil, demons, dark magic, and nightmares.

Epic Fantasy – These stories usually follow a traditional hero who is caught up in a battle of Good versus Evil.

Mythology – Stories that feature foreign, mystical worlds with strange heroes and creatures, not unlike faerie tales.

Historical Fantasy – Historical fantasy is set in actual historical eras but contains fantasy elements.

Magic Realism – Fantasy stories in which magic is an accepted part of the world.

Humorous Fantasy – Fantasy stories with comedic undertones.

Science Fiction Fantasy – Stories involving technological or scientific elements.

Swords and Sorcery – These stories often have medieval undertones and feature heroic characters whose weapon of choice is the sword.

Choose your World

The **setting** of your book is important to choose early on, because it will serve as the world in which your story plays out. One of the best things about a setting is that it can range from plain and simple to highly complex. One of the most fun and exciting parts of writing fantasy is that you can go all out and create an entire world, completely designed by you. You have the freedom to make your world any way you want. J. R. R. Tolkien, Frank L. Baum and J.K. Rowling among other famous fantasy writers have taken advantage of this component and created amazing and enchanting worlds.

If you are going to set your fantasy story in an imaginary world, it is your job as the author to truly bring that world to life for your readers. You must describe your imaginary world well if you hope to convince your readers that the setting actually exists somewhere, or at least suspend their disbelief for the duration of the story.. The key to successful world-crafting is to be highly descriptive and detail-oriented. Creating a world from a completely blank slate can be pretty challenging, so here are some questions that can get you started:

- What color is the sky?

- What is the atmosphere like?

- What kind of plant life exists?

- What kind of creatures lives in the world?

- What is the geography of the world?

- Is your world set on a different planet?

- Is your world set in a spaceship or other non-planet entity?

- What kind of architecture is reflected in the buildings?

- Does it rain/snow/storm there?

- What is the average outside temperature?

- Are the weather/seasons consistent?

- How do characters travel?

- Are there animals in your world?

- What raw resources are used for building/fueling?

Time and Date – Set a clear era for your book to inhabit; this will help your readers visualize your story. Some authors choose to draw out a timeline in their books, but that step is highly optional. At any rate, it is important to state or at least hint at the age in which your book is set so that readers have an idea of how your characters will dress, act, and talk. Once you have set your timeframe, you will need to check periodically for time discrepancies. For example, if your book is set in the 1800's, your characters cannot just whip out their cell phones and exchange phone numbers. That would never happen in a fantasy world. When I am writing historical fiction, I like to use actual dates in my chapter names, to give my readers a feel for the passage of time. Although the majority of historical fantasy stories are set during medieval times or in the past, contemporary fantasy can be set in modern times.

Atmosphere – The atmosphere of your setting helps to set various moods within your story. You can use the weather, the lighting, or some other external factor to set the mood, but do so sparingly. I've heard that publishers are turned off by stories that start by describing the weather. Work the atmosphere into your story by describing it rather than by telling the details. For example, if the atmosphere is intended to be dark and sinister, instead of saying, "It was really dark and ghosts screamed in the background", you could more tactfully say your main character "peers uneasily into the pitch dark night, all the more nervous because he is unable to see the source of the evil laughter that seems to surround him."

Geography – The geography of your setting can help frame the action in your story. Geography includes climate, plant life, bodies of water, and other land masses. Perhaps your main character is a hunter who lives in the tall, isolated mountains. Or, maybe your story is a fairy tale set in the middle of the woods, where the main characters chop down trees for firewood.

I didn't think geography mattered at first, but it really does. Describing geography is especially important in fantasy, which has a tendency to include scenes and settings in woods, caves, mountains, beaches and other nature spots. This is all the more essential if that wood or beach is in a world you imagined. Better describe the geographical setting thoroughly. Otherwise, your readers will read the story against an empty backdrop.

Historical Context – If your story revolves around an important historical event, such as a war or a tsunami, include that event in your setting. This will anchor the story in time for your readers.

Politics, Economics, Sociology, Religion – These factors play into your setting and can dramatically affect the behaviors and the personality of your characters. A character from a poor family will likely differ from a character who comes from an affluent family. Considering these factors can also help you with set up the conflict. You have a built-in conflict brewing if your character is raised in a high-status background, but finds himself living in a slum. Brainstorm some ideas surrounding these contexts and see what conflicts or plot twists you can come up with. Here are some good questions that you can ask to get started:

- Does your world have a social structure?

- What is the currency of your world?

- What are the politics of your world?

- Does your world have a leader?

- What type of leadership does your world utilize?

- Do those who live in your world follow a religion?

- What do your people do for work?

- What rituals do your characters follow?

- What is the fashion style of your characters?

- What do your characters do for recreation?

- What kind of art/music do your characters like?

- What types of work do your characters perform?

Your book's physical setting can be complex, affecting even minor details, such as mannerisms, food or language. Setting can also be effective when it is kept to a few stark specifics. You can use subtle or lavish amounts of imagination, although I personally prefer the risk of erring in excess.

Research your world thoroughly, if you're not creating it from scratch. For example, if you plan to set your story in New York City, I highly recommend spending at least a day there to get a feel for what goes on, in addition to looking it up in newspaper articles and YouTube videos. Even if you are from New York and know every borough intimately, I suggest you take a day to play tourist, giving yourself a chance to view the old and familiar through fresh eyes.

World Building [Factors of a Great Novel #2] by Katytastic is an excellent supplemental video to watch for more tips on world building.

What Makes Your Story Interesting?

One of your goals as a writer should be to write a story that will reach out and grab the interest of your readers. Picture them picking up your book and just dying to turn each page to find out what happens next. However, for that to happen, your book must be interesting, with fully fleshed out characters and a well-rounded story arc.

First, you should think about the plot. What is your plot? What kind of plot twists do you want to use? A good plot contains **exposition** (background descriptions to set the story and introduce the plot), **rising action** (the events, conflicts, increasing tension, twists and turns that lead to the high point of the story), a **climax** (the high point, where conflict elements really hit the fan), **falling action** (resolution of ongoing conflicts, filling in gaps that would otherwise leave your audience hanging in suspense) and a **resolution** (bringing the story to a satisfying end).

Additionally, your story should have an early **hook**, something to swiftly engage your reader and make them want to read more. I've been advised to open my stories with some sort of disturbance, because a well-written disturbance automatically piques reader curiosity and raises questions about the back-story, the characters, and their motives. Your hook can be as intense as two characters engaged in a swordfight, but it may also appear in more subtle form, such as a distressed mother trying to find a toddler who is lost in the woods. One way to determine if your story has a good hook is to see if it leaves readers wanting to know what happens next. For example, a book that opens up with a missing toddler would probably make readers ask, "Will the mother find the toddler? Will she accidentally stumble upon a discovery? Will something exciting happen?"

Create a Plot Twist

Plot twists are essential to sustaining reader interest. You want to ensure that your story is not boring but also avoid it becoming unbelievable. So, how do you go about creating a good plot twist? When one friend was writing her first novel, she was stumped for the longest time about how to make her story intriguing. Then one day, as she was taking a walk, a plot twist just popped into her mind out of nowhere. Some writers get lucky that way, but if your plot twist doesn't come to you like a gift, I have a few exercises that may help stimulate some ideas.

One powerful exercise is to brainstorm a list of possible–and impossible–plot twists. Write down at least ten ideas. Then, consider each idea no matter how implausible; even crazy ideas can sometime spawn brilliant ones.

Another suggestion is to read your story, looking for scenes that might contain potential clues to a plot twist. For example, my friend originally wrote a scene in which her two main characters, a pair of former lovers, met up on a street corner, after having no contact for over three years. During their conversation, the female character mentioned she had some news to share. However, before she had a chance to let it out, the two got into an argument and the woman left without revealing her secret. That scene contained plenty of wiggle room for the author to experiment with until she could figure out how to use the untold secret as the setup for a major plot twist.

It helps to develop two or three plot twists, each leading into the next one. An easy way to do this is to follow a basic **three act structure** for your book. In this structure, your story will have a beginning, middle, and an end. Set your hook and create tension in the beginning of the story with the first twist, using some type of challenge, obstacle, or disturbance. In this section, make extensive use of exposition and dialogue to introduce your readers to the setting and the main characters.

In the middle of your story, insert another twist. Make it a little more dramatic than the first one. Let this plot twist serve as the "point of no return" for your main character. Once he or she encounters this twist, there is nowhere to go but forward. Make this plot twist life-changing. This part, the middle of your book, should take up the majority of your content.

Toward the end of the middle section, insert your third plot twist, which will lead directly to the climax, the beginning of the end. This challenge or obstacle should ultimately lead to the resolution of all the individual threads in your story. In the climax, your protagonist will often be called on to make some sort of decision. In many fantasy stories, this twist will set up the final confrontation, either between two characters or within the main character. You must clearly show whether or not your main character has accomplished the goal set out earlier in the book. You may choose any type of ending. Although many readers look forward to a happy ending, sometimes your story will call for one that is sad or bittersweet.

Inference

Narrative summary, a simple recitation of actions and the explicit statement of emotions or motives, makes for a boring, flat novel. If you leave nothing unsaid, you will be cheating your reader's imagination. That is why I say **show, don't tell**. Let your readers exist inside the story, viewing their surroundings as they view real life. In real life, nobody is handed all the information; most of the time, we have to infer motives and emotions by observing the circumstances in our larger environment. For example, take a look at the two passages below and ask yourself which one sounds better:

Passage A – John ran swiftly through the forest. Behind him, an army of elves were quickly catching up. Their faces were angry and they wielded swords and other weapons in their hand. A few steps ahead of him, a river separated the rest of the land. He had nowhere else to go.

Passage B – His chest heavy and burning, John swiftly ran through the forest, not bothering to note the cuts and scrapes inflicted by the brambles. Nervously looking over his shoulder, he could see a swarm of elves, wielding sharp, pointed swords and other murderous weapons. His heart pounding, he silently told himself, "Got to get out of sight, got to disappear." His getaway plan was promptly interrupted as his feet skidded down the muddy bank of a large, frothing river that separated him from the land ahead. His heart dropped. He was trapped.

Both passages made available the basic facts. However, the second paragraph sounds a lot better, right? You can actually *feel* the nervousness and tension of the main character through the description of his physical experience. As you read about the burning chest, fresh scrapes, and the drop in his heart, you actually start to feel the tension along with the character. You have successfully put yourself in the character's shoes.

I'll bet the second paragraph also held your interest a lot better than the first one. Readers don't like to trudge through text that is boring and dragged out. Think of it this way: If you were a college student, would you select a class under a professor who stands in front of the class and speaks in a monotone, or would you prefer one who moves around and puts some zest into his lecture?

Notice how the second paragraph employs multiple senses in its description of the action. Touch, taste, sight, sound, and smell are powerful senses in real life; they can be just as useful when writing a story. Take note of how I used the senses of sight and touch to enhance the second paragraph. If you were to use taste, you could take a flat sentence such as "the chocolate cake with vanilla icing tasted good" and convert it to, "Warm, gooey chocolate dripped out of the freshly baked cake as it sat on the platter, waiting to be topped off with sweet vanilla icing." Which sentence makes your mouth drool?

Mechanics are Important

Use correct spelling, Standard English grammar, and appropriate punctuation in your story. Exceptions are only allowed when slang phrases suit your environment or when you have a character who speaks with an accent. There's nothing more annoying than trying to read a book containing multiple errors; every mistake is a slap in the face of a reader. Always pay a proofreader to take a last look at your work before sending it off; you need a fresh set of eyes to see what you can't and the small price is well worth paying for the peace of mind you gain.

If you plan to publish your tale as an eBook, take the time to ensure that your book is formatted correctly for all platforms. Again, there's nothing worse than downloading a book and not being able to read it smoothly on your screen. Improper formatting only makes your text harder to follow; you also run the risk of your readers requesting a refund and leaving a bad review in their wake.

Chapter 3: Developing Fantasy Characters

Carefully developed characters are probably the most important element to crafting an interesting fantasy story. When writing fantasy, it is easy to get lost in describing the setting or focusing *too* much on the plot without giving much thought to your characters. Characters are the heartbeat of your book; they drive your plot forward and, when your readers fully identify with a character, it helps them fully immerse in the story. Since they are so important, you'll need to know how to create fully-developed, dynamic characters for your story. This chapter will show you how.

Choose Your Major Characters

How many characters belong in one story? There really is no concrete answer. At minimum, you'll need at least one character, your main character, who can be a protagonist, antagonist, or antihero. Most fantasy novels have at least one protagonist and one antagonist. If you only have one character, then his or her opponent in conflict will likely be the inner self, although some survival stories feature natural phenomena as the antagonist.

Protagonist

A protagonist is the central character of your book, also known as a central character, major character, a dynamic or a round character. This main character must be one with whom your readers can identify. A protagonist is never perfect; in fact, your character's flaws are often what create the story's conflict. You will probably put a lot of effort into creating and understanding your protagonist. He or she must be as true-to-life as possible; after all, this is who your readers will follow throughout the entire story. Let your central character develop and grow across the span of your story. Readers like to watch a protagonist undergo substantial change; this is what they experience in their own lives. Keep in mind that your readers are often drawn to a book because they are hungry to learn how another person solved a problem that is similar to their own.

I find that making your protagonist as true to life and as detailed as possible can help make him live in the minds of your readers. I do this by answering as many questions as possible about my protagonist. For example, I ask myself:

- Where does my character live? With whom does he live?

- What type of dwelling does he live in? How did he come to live there? Does he like it?

- Where is he originally from? What is his background?

- How old is my protagonist? (This is a very important question, because it determines so many other details).

- What is my protagonist's name? How does this reflect his personality, his background, and even possibly, the challenge he will face in this book?

- What is the social class of my protagonist?

- What does my protagonist look like? (The more detailed a description, the better).

- What was his childhood like and how does it affect him now?

- What does my protagonist do for work? What makes up a typical day?

- How does my protagonist handle change/conflict?

- What kind of relationships does he have?

- What is his goal?

Let these questions branch off into sub-questions. For example, when you ask yourself about your protagonist's childhood, explore whether he was raised by a single mother, by an abusive father, or by adoptive parents. By answering these questions, you are creating a solid framework for your book. For example, if you decide that your protagonist is a sixteen-year-old boy, you wouldn't write a scene with him drinking in a bar unless you're painting him as a defiant teen or if that is the culture in your fantasy world. Avoid letting your protagonist live an unchanging and boring life; otherwise you will not hold your readers' attention long enough for them to reach the checkout lane.

Describe Your Protagonist Early

It is crucial for your readers to get acquainted with your protagonist early in the story; otherwise, they will be less likely to identify places where inner growth and change may occur. Think of your story's beginning as a snapshot of your protagonist in his or her "lost" state or in status quo. Ensure that your readers understand who your protagonist is at the beginning, so they will better comprehend the changes, challenges, sacrifices and obstacles he will go through en route to becoming a more "complete" person. For example, let's review the storyline from the movie *Shrek*. In the beginning, Shrek was a miserable, lonely monster who had no friends and projected a generally negative attitude. However, by the end, the events, challenges, and friendships he experienced had changed him into a happily married, positive-thinking monster. The ending wouldn't have been significant at all if Shrek had remained unchanged.

Here are some additional questions to focus on once you've settled on the basics of your protagonist:

- Which external factors act as a stimulus for which internal factors? In other words, what happens around your protagonist and what goes on inside his head as a result? If your protagonist is a generally moral person, but he loses his home and is forced to live in a cave, where might that lead?

  The conflict between external circumstance and internal morals will be the drawing factor of your book. Your protagonist is faced with a choice: will he violate his morals by breaking the law to survive, something he would have never done earlier, or will he discover another way out of his dilemma?

- What will be the trigger that moves your protagonist to change? Perhaps she is required to overcome a specific character weakness in order to achieve "completeness." Another main character may suddenly, in an "aha" moment, discover he now knows what is happening or he now has what he needs to emerge from his difficulty. This sudden knowledge will often trigger your final plot twist and lead directly to the climax of your story.

- Why is it significant for your protagonist to reach "completeness?" To answer this question, think in terms of life lessons. Readers like to feel your story has a message; in many cases this theme will come as a moral or a life lesson that becomes apparent by the end of the story. For example, the life lesson in *Hansel and Gretel* is to never take candy from strangers. The two protagonists are completely unaware of this advice until they've survived a terrible experience as a result of taking candy from a stranger. Odds are, if a sequel to that fairy tale was ever written, Hansel and Gretel would probably display a healthy distrust toward strangers bearing candy.

- What will cause the protagonist to become complete by the end? The answer to this question is often a high-stakes climax followed by an engaging victory. Think of it as "the final standoff" or a life-changing event that firmly establishes the resolution. For example, in *The Wizard of Oz*, Dorothy finally gets her chance to go home. However, she fails to make it into the balloon with the wizard, so poor Dorothy–along with the waiting public–thinks she's stuck in Oz forever. When she clicks her heels three times and wakes up in her own bed, Dorothy realizes how grateful she is for her family, because she thought she had lost them forever. Because of the double scare, Dorothy will never again resent her "boring" existence.

- Does your protagonist gain redemption in the end? Will he be required to sacrifice something to reach his goal? Hero figures often make a major sacrifice before they can succeed. In a traditional hero story, the hero often sacrifices his or her life for the good of the people, but it doesn't have to play out that way. In the first *Spiderman* movie, Peter Parker sacrifices his chance for a relationship with M.J., in order to protect his identity and continue to protect the people. Readers like to see a protagonist make a sacrifice, because it is inspiring. Your character gives up something he values in order to benefit somebody else.

Alternatively, your protagonist may be an **Anti-Hero**. An anti-hero protagonist does not have the traditional positive qualities of a regular protagonist and is often immoral, self-centered, or unheroic. Some anti-heroes have addictions or are involved in some sort of corruption. However, an anti-hero usually grows into a more complete person by the end of the story, even though that growth often comes at the cost of his life. Anti-heroes often inspire readers to overcome their own insecurities.

A Well-rounded Protagonist

Good protagonists should contain enough detail of character to make them interesting individuals. Here are some points to consider:

First of all, your protagonist needs a **personality**; otherwise you're drawing with a white crayon on white paper, so to speak. You want your protagonist to jump off the page and into the hearts of your readers. The best way to create a strong personality is to answer as many questions as you can about his background. You'll want to be able to explain and predict your protagonist's thoughts and feelings.

Exercises

You can increase your personality development skills by participating in method acting classes or stream of consciousness exercises. The activity below may also be of help:

I'm a big fan of voice recorders; I think talking into a voice recorder as if you were your protagonist can be a very helpful creative exercise. To experience this exercise, begin by introducing yourself and then speak as if you were that character and see what comes out. Try this for at least ten minutes, since you will need a little time to get used to the concept and really get into your character. Your brain could very well start making up things you think are genius. When you are finished, replay the tape to glean the best parts for your protagonist.

A good way to add some personality to your protagonist is to **exploit her fear**. Just because your protagonist isn't real doesn't mean she can't feel fear. We all have fears; just connect your protagonist's fears to the story line. This will help your character seem more real and believable. A fearless protagonist (unless it makes sense in the story) will all too often come across as robotic and nonhuman.

You also need to decide what your protagonist's **internal conflict** will be. Internal conflict is when your character wants two things but is unsure which one to pick or how to get both. The best way to capture your readers' attention and take them on a psychological joyride is to create an internal conflict that is emotional and testing. Try to stay near to a type of internal conflict you might find in yourself one day.

Once you've figured out the internal conflict, you'll also want to determine the **external conflict.** External conflict is driven by an outside factor that is somehow related to the internal conflict. For example, internal conflict is when your protagonist has to pick between fleeing his hometown and remaining in an unhealthy and unsafe environment. If you add in an assassin who is chasing your protagonist, that will serve as your external conflict.

Next, your protagonist needs **motivation.** A character's motivation is usually connected to her values and ambitions as well as her goals. A good way to portray motivation in your story is to give your protagonist two clashing values, which will create internal conflict; then your character will be forced to pick between them. Ambition, which represents what your protagonist wants more than anything, will be the driving motivation. Limit your protagonist's ambition to one thing. Her ambition will move her to choose between options and can be the driving force behind her actions.

Your protagonist should also have **relationships** with other characters in your story. Most often, your protagonist will have an existing relationship with the antagonist, as well as with minor characters; all relationships can help push your story forward. A lone ranger protagonist can easily dry up very quickly, unless he has other people in his life. Relationships make it possible for your protagonist to connect with your readers. Your audience wants to identify with the main character; that's one of the main reasons people read books in the first place. For example, young adult books are specifically written for young adults, with characters of the same age who experience conflicts similar to those of a typical young adult.

Give your protagonist a unique **voice.** This often includes the way your character speaks and moves. For example, if your protagonist is n orc, he might talk using orc jargon or broken English. If your protagonist is a professor of magic, she would probably speak with advanced vocabulary and complex sentence structures. Giving your protagonist a unique voice helps establish your main character's personality. It can even reflect part of a backstory. For example, if your character stutters, his voice could link to a past that involved bullying or abuse.

Similarly, your protagonist should be full of **emotion.** An emotionless protagonist is worse than watching paint dry. For example, if your protagonist is in the middle of a break-up with someone else, think about what emotions will come into play. Often the other person will be extremely upset and will cry, beg, or otherwise try to convince your protagonist not to walk away. All the while, the main character is resistant to these emotions and just wants out of the relationship once and for all. In another scenario, think about all of the emotions present in a wedding scene. The feelings would be mostly positive, but think about a parent's objection or something else that could go wrong. Examine many possible scenarios and use their related emotions to your advantage when you write.

Give your protagonist at least one **strength** and one **flaw.** A protagonist with no strengths at all is pretty boring and one-dimensional. So is one with no flaws. What's the point of reading about your protagonist if he or she doesn't have anything human to offer or leave space for personal growth? If you give your protagonist an amazing strength, also include a character flaw. The juxtaposition of these two character traits opens up all sorts of possibilities to generate conflict. For example, your character in a love story could be a genius in the sword fighting arena, but at the same time be horribly clumsy when it comes to dating.

What else makes for a good protagonist? One key is inclusion of a **mystery** or a **secret.** This works best if one character is already mysterious and another one has a secret; the secret may explain why the other character is so mysterious. For example, let's say you are writing a story about a love triangle, in which your protagonist skips town with the woman of his dreams but still stays in touch with his ex. The ex has a secret; she is carrying his child, or she has some sort of incurable disease. The new girlfriend doesn't know this secret, so her boyfriend's mystique drives her crazy. If your readers don't know the secret either, they will be driven crazy as well and are all the more likely to read to the end of your book in their quest to uncover the secret.

The majority of readers like to see a protagonist with lots of courage, inner strength, sex appeal, mental sharpness, generosity, kindness, or selflessness. However, fiction is fiction, so it's totally up to you and your story, what kind of person you want your protagonist to be. Of course, if your protagonist is an anti-hero, you won't make him selfless or genuinely caring.

One of the best things about fiction is that following these rules is somewhat optional. I say "somewhat" because you must know the rules thoroughly before you can understand when you can get away with bending, or outright breaking them. Nine times out of ten, it is best to stick closely to the rules if you want to be successful, but you know what they say about rules being built to be broken. There's really no straight answer. You could play by the rules and write a flop; you could also deviate from them and discover you've captured your audience with a completely new concept.

While we have focused on developing a powerful protagonist you can apply all of these tools to your other characters; for a successful book, you need a well-rounded cast. If your protagonist is fully developed but is surrounded by flat, one-dimensional characters, you'll still have a weak storyline.

Side Note: Creating Conflict in Fantasy

It is super important to pay attention to how you develop your protagonist's conflict when writing fantasy. Since it is such a creative, open-minded genre, it is easy to get lost within the depths of your imagination and focus more on your story world and its inhabitants rather than the actual conflict at hand. However, the conflict of your story is what will capture your readers' attention and serve as a powerful emotions driver, making it the most important factor in your book. In any type of fiction, your protagonist will grow and develop between the beginning and end of your story; fantasy is no exception. Even if the characters in your story are not human, you must remember that your readers are, and you will have to make a relatable connection.

Antagonist

The antagonist is a character in your story that goes up against the protagonist. He or she usually stirs up conflict, sometimes just by entering the scene. In the majority of fantasy stories the antagonist is very clear, but in others it's not as easy to pick out. Think of the antagonist as the personification of an obstacle your protagonist must overcome. Sometimes the antagonist is referred to as the **foil**, which describes the antagonist as a contrasting character, in terms of personal qualities.

In fantasy stories, it is common for the antagonist to be non-human. There are three general types of non-human antagonists: **creatures, environment, and social issues.**

While some creatures are human-like, there are a slew of unique creatures such as dragons, sea dwellers and other animalistic beings that can also serve as an antagonist. In this context, the creatures attack the protagonist simply because of its instincts–for example, a sea dweller haunts the ocean simply because it was designed to be that way–but it still poses a considerable danger to the protagonist, providing the conflict. Creatures can also be controlled by an external antagonist who uses them for evil purposes. For example, a villain with magical powers might turn all the forest animals into vicious man-eaters so he can easily take over the town.

The environment of the story can also serve as an antagonist. Destructive but natural forces such as the weather or phenomena like twisters and earthquakes can create a disturbance that antagonizes the protagonist. Even a foreign land itself can be the antagonist. For example, Dorothy was resistant to Oz and just wanted to get home to Kansas.

A social issue can serve as an antagonist as well. Think about things such as racism, gender differences, social class inequalities, or sexism. All of these things can pose a barrier for your protagonist. Perhaps a young hunter wants to join the elves army but is discriminated against because he is human and not elf. Or a peasant believes he has what it takes to marry the princess of the kingdom. The possibilities are endless when it comes to using social issues as antagonists.

Minor Characters

These are characters that assist in moving the story forward or serve as a contrasting personality. They can provide depth to more important characters by opening up backstory elements. **Stock Characters** are flat, stereotypical individuals who are easily identified, such as the mad scientist or the nerd. However, use stock characters sparingly. A story peopled by stock characters can seem cartoonish and is difficult to elevate beyond boring. Here are some common fantasy archetypes for you to experiment with:

The Mentor – In a fantasy story, a mentor character is often indispensable in helping the protagonist develop and move forward. The mentor is often useful for invoking emotions, because he often leaves the protagonist to fend for himself. The tension created by this abandonment can also be used as a plot point. Include a mentor when he is essential to the shape of your story.

The Sidekick – A sidekick character is helpful for bringing along elements such as advice, humor or differing opinions to the story. Sidekicks can be significant (like Ron and Hermione from *Harry Potter*) or less significant but nonetheless an important component of the fantasy story. A sidekick can help make your protagonist more relatable.

The Love Interest – A love interest can also make your protagonist more relevant to your readers. Your love interest can initiate plot points and drive suspense. The best way to portray the relationship between a love interest and the protagonist in a fantasy story is to treat it like a relationship in any other genre. You want this relationship to be as realistic as possible, to draw in your readers.

Deus ex Machina Characters

Deus ex Machina is a term that literally means "God from the machine." It is a plot device borrowed from Ancient Greece in which the main characters from a story are suddenly rescued by a character or force that appears out of thin air. This generally happens when the main characters are in a position in which it seems unlikely that there is another way out.

In other types of fiction writing, it is very risky to use Deus ex Machina, because readers often believe the author is just doing it to be lazy. However, you can get away with this in fantasy, due to the extensive suspension of disbelief created by the genre. For example, if your story is set in a world with giant friendly flying dinosaurs, it would be believable for a giant friendly flying dinosaur to come save your protagonist from of a near-death situation. Another example is when your protagonist suddenly remembers the magical item in his pocket designed to protect him from the current danger.

As long as your Deus ex Machina situation fits within the context of your fantasy story, I would say it's safe to use. Let's say you were actually writing a historic Elizabethan romance and a giant friendly flying dinosaur came and saved everybody; now that would be an example of the author being lazy and "cheating" because there's nothing about a historical romance that would incorporate those kinds of creatures. If you're writing a suspense thriller set in modern times, your protagonist cannot suddenly pull out a magic item to save everybody from harm. Such things just aren't believable in that genre. However, it *is* a normal part of fantasy, so have some fun with this tool!

When writing fantasy, you might want to include a Deus ex Machina character, even if you're not planning to go down that route. It's always good to have a character like that on hand, just in case you can't think of anywhere else to take your plot or if you happen to think of an epic way to use him. It also can keep your readers guessing, if you have this kind of character hanging around. To incorporate this character, review the context of your story and create someone to fit within that context.

One Main Question, One Main Goal

As I mentioned earlier, your story should have a single main question, which usually connects with the goal of your protagonist. For example, Indiana Jones usually goes off looking for treasure, which provokes the readers to ask, "Will he find the treasure?" Your story may generate multiple questions, but one should always be primary.

To ensure that your round characters stay round, every character should have a goal. The most important goals are usually the conflicting objectives that strike sparks between your protagonist and antagonist. For example, Spiderman (the protagonist) wants to protect the city while the Green Goblin (the antagonist) wants to destroy him—and it. Spiderman also wants M. J. (a minor character) to fall in love with him, while she is more focused on becoming an actress. People who watch the movie find themselves asking questions about both unknowns. Notice how all three of these characters have goals that help move the story forward.

Naming Your Fantasy Character

One of the most fun things about fantasy writing is that you can be extra creative with the names of your characters. Creative character names can be seen in famous fantasy books such as *The Hobbit, The Lord of the Rings* trilogy and *Harry Potter*, to name a few. Of course, the names of the characters in your fantasy story can be modern, such as Queen Susan or King Edmund, in *The Chronicles of Narnia* (by C. S. Lewis), but many authors opt for more "interesting" names. So how do you go about creatively naming a fantasy character?

One strategy is to analyze your character's qualities and derive the name from there. In *Pokemon*, for example, Squirtle is the name of a magical turtle that is famously known for squirting water out of its mouth. Naming a character after his or her qualities can help you strengthen his or her identity. You could also name your character as an homage to another character in fantasy literature or folklore.

A second strategy is to consider your character's relation to the setting. If your story is set on another planet, it is highly unlikely that he or she will have a modern earthly name. It is more likely to sound galactic or futuristic. If your story is set on a low-class farm, your character will probably have a more common, less exotic name.

Try to avoid the super obvious, such as naming a good guy "Angel" and the bad guy "Lucifer."

You will want to keep the names of your characters consistent. You don't want to give a few characters really creative names, but leave the rest with mundane earthly names. Characters in the same ethnic background should all have names that sound like their ethnicity. Of course, use logic in making this decision. If your story is about a character who lived in the 1990's and time traveled to the year 6000, it would make sense for him to have a name that fits his place of origin.

Also, ensure that the creative name you pick is pronounceable. An unpronounceable name is quite distracting; it can take your reader's focus away from the plot. If you're not sure whether readers will be able to instinctively pronounce the name, I recommend providing the proper pronunciation in a note.

If I'm completely stumped when hunting down a good name for a character, one strategy I use is to look up names and their respective meanings. A good resource for this is a baby names website; on it you can find an abundance of names from a variety of cultures and religions. I often browse through a site, looking at the meanings of the names, ultimately choosing a name that reflects the personality of my character.

You can combine two names to give your character a highly complex meaning. You can also use Latin or Greek to create a meaningful name. For example, Draco Malfoy, an antagonist in *Harry Potter,* has a highly descriptive name. "Mal" is a Latin prefix meaning "bad." I like to use street names for the last names of my characters because some street names are quite interesting. For example, I used to drive past a street called "Barkalow Avenue" and I often thought to myself, "That's going to be the surname of one of my characters."

Finally, if you really, really can't come up with anything, you could use an online fantasy name generator to get some ideas. These generators are often used by people who play RPGs (role-playing games) or MMORPGs (massively multiplayer online role-playing games), but there's no harm in using them to pick a character's name for your book.

Character History

It is not uncommon to have characters of several races or species in fantasy stories. When that is the case, it is important to fully develop the history of both races or species. As the author, you will need to know things such as how the species in your story interact with each other, if any inter-racial tensions exist, and how both came to be. The more prominently the race or species figures in your story, the broader and more developed their history should be. For example, if you have gnomes in your story who pretty much stay in the background, you do not need to know as much about them as you would about the fish-people who are the focus of the story.

I recommend writing your characters' histories in a separate document you can keep handy for reference.

Keep a Character List

I also highly recommend creating and maintaining a character list to prevent and inconsistencies in your story. For example, if you write in the beginning that your character has brown eyes, you don't want to describe her eyes as blue a few chapters later. A detailed character list that includes physical characteristics, mental traits, and a personal background will remind you at a glance that your character has brown eyes. My artistic capability scarcely extends beyond stick figures, but if you can draw, I highly recommend setting down a highly detailed visual representation of your characters, especial the primaries.

Backstory

Alright, let's talk more about the backstory. Backstories can serve as a useful tool to flesh out your various personalities. A character's backstory is what helps your readers understand where he is coming from—quite literally, what causes her to drop to the ground whenever lightening explodes, or why he carries that enormous chip on his shoulder. It is essentially the history of your character. Although your protagonist's backstory is often the most important, all your characters can become more realistic if hints to their backstories are dropped periodically.

One mistake I have made—and had to repent from—is to focus so strongly on a single character's backstory that I fail to focus on the development of the plot. The strongest character in the world cannot overcome a lame plot.

Also, don't make the mistake of turning your first few chapters into a backstory. A backstory is just that, an entirely separate story. Call it a prequel if you will, but only publish it *after* your current novel has become successful!

Flashbacks are a useful tool to reveal aspects of a character's backstory. I know one author who has utilized flashbacks to complement what she was actually writing and it worked out well. What she did was to start telling the main story about a girl who was kidnapped, then she sprinkled snippets of backstory throughout the book in the form of flashbacks. As you read through the book, you learn what the girl had been doing prior to being snatched, and you also discover why her abductors were so crazy as to nab her. Flashbacks not only help round out the characters, they also keep the readers' curiosity piqued for new information.

If you're going to use flashbacks to tell your story, be careful to transition smoothly back and forth between them and your story's present tense. One straightforward method is to start a flashback as a new scene, indicating it by using the simple past tense. When you end the flashback, close out the scene and switch back to the present tense, continuing the main story.

The delightful thing about a backstory is that you can either create it up front or develop it as you go along. I find that having a general idea of a character's backstory is good enough for starters; you can flesh out the details as you write. Having even a rough backstory written out in front of you helps you keep track of your story's context. This is especially useful if you have an extensive backstory for multiple characters.

I recommend using backstory development as a warm-up for additional writing. Just select a character and start developing a backstory. Don't worry; your backstory can evolve as your story develops. Then, as you write your main book, you can decide what snippets or details from the backstory will help move your story forward.

Interior Monologue

Knowing how to use interior monologue (essentially getting into the head of your character) is highly useful. There are two types of interior monologue–direct and indirect. Direct interior monologue is when your character is speaking directly from inside her head. Many authors use italics to indicate this, as in this example:

"The morning sunlight shone down on the forest. Prince John was taking a leisurely stroll through the woods now that the rain had finally stopped. Once he reached the end of the trail, he stopped and took a deep breath. *I love that fresh, just-rained smell of the woods.*"

Direct interior monologue is also best written in first person present tense, as you can see in the example above. Putting direct thoughts in italics helps them stand out to the reader. That being said, you should try to use italicized direct interior monologue sparingly, otherwise it will lose its special flavor.

Indirect interior monologue exists when the author tells you a character's inner thoughts as narrative description, as seen in this example:

"Being in love with a common farm girl was something that Prince John kept quiet. It scared him to think how his affluent parents would react."

Sometimes, a tag, such as "he said" or "she thought" is necessary to keep straight who is thinking what. For example:

"*I have been angry ever since I learned we can't see each other*, he thought to himself."

Most authors I know use a mixture of direct and indirect interior monologue to reveal their characters' internal processing. People sometimes read fiction because the interior monologue enables them to see what a character is thinking, as opposed to guessing from the action, as in a movie.

Interior emotions can help develop your character. Interior emotion tells readers about your character by showing their emotions. For example, if your character is scared, you can describe the physical effects of fear such as starting to sweat, or a racing heart. Don't come right out and say that he's scared. That's narrative summary, something I already warned you to avoid for the most part. If you are unsure how to work interior emotion into your scene, just ask yourself, "What is my character feeling and what does that look like?" Similes and metaphors can add power to your descriptions of interior emotion. Just use highly clichéd examples very sparingly.

How Does Your Creature Really Feel?

Since most fantasy stories feature creatures other than humans, it is important to really put yourself in your characters' shoes and look at things from their perspectives, in order to make your story as realistic as possible. For example, it is simply not enough to write an elf character similar to a human character. When dealing with characters of a different species or race, there are a few important questions to keep nearby that will help shape them:

1. How long has your character or its species lived? If a character has lived for thousands of years then it is likely he, she or it has seen many things over the years and has a unique perspective compared to humans or other species.

2. How will certain events affect your character or its species? For example, a dry spell in the land may not affect human characters, who are able to adapt to those conditions, but how would it affect other creatures who live in a wet habitat?

3. What are the values of your characters or their species? Just as different cultures and races in the real world have differing values, the same can go for creatures in a fantasy story. A good example of this can be found in the movie *The Goonies*. One of the characters, a creature named Sloth, is with the antagonists of the film but in the end, he ends up befriending and saving the protagonists, because he didn't agree with the other antagonists who were trying to harm them.

Developing Character Through Dialogue

Dialogue is a high priority in fiction because it helps develop your characters and push your plot forward. That being said, the dialogue in your book must be perfectly crafted. Alfred Hitchcock once said that a good story is "life with the dull parts taken out." In other words, readers don't want to read something like this:

"What do you want for lunch today? Some fresh herbs?"
"Oh yeah, that sounds good."
"Okay, I'll go gather some right now."

Boring, right? Dialogue requires focus, impact, and relevance to be effective. It needs to push your plot forward or reveal something about your characters. For example, let's rewrite the above example to create some conflict and introduce tension between the characters:

"What do you want for lunch today? Some fresh herbs?"
"All you ever feed me is herbs. You never let me pick what *I* want to eat. A fresh buffalo sounds better."
"If you're going to be so picky about the food we eat, maybe you should get a job as a hunter so you can bring home your own food."

Writing Creatures – Screenwriting Fantasy and Horror Characters from the Stan Winston School provides additional helpful insights on how to create and develop characters for a fantasy book.

Chapter 4: Fantasy Story Goals

Before you can even start writing, it helps to have an inkling about the point of your story. An idea essentially says "somebody does something interesting" or "something exciting happens," but an idea is not a fully fleshed out novel. After you come up with your idea, you'll need to start filling in the blanks. Who is that somebody? What happens that is so exciting? This chapter is all about how to figure that out.

The goal of a story is often echoed in the protagonist's goal, so it only makes sense to first figure out what your protagonist wants. Think about internal and external goals and how conflict can play into them. Let's say that you have an idea to write a book about pirates that actually do good instead of evil. That's your idea. Now you have to flesh out the details. Say there is one pirate named Johnny, he's your protagonist and he is the one who is behind this change in behavior. Why? Maybe because he met a girl and wants to exit the life of a pirate. We can add conflict by providing background information that explains when Johnny first became a pirate, he took a lifelong vow; now a fellow pirate is determined to prevent Johnny from weaseling out of his promise. See how the fleshing out process works? The story goal in this case could be something like, "escape evil and live free."

Here are some examples of classic fantasy story goals that you might be able to work into your idea:

Good versus Evil

The good versus evil premise is probably the top story goal in fantasy writing, as it serves as the underlying basis for some of the most popular fantasy novels on the market. In a story where the theme is good versus evil, there is usually a protagonist who usually starts out as an everyday, normal character but discovers that he or she is the "chosen" one to fulfill a destiny or go on a quest, usually to abolish something evil once and for all. These types of stories often have a clearly defined protagonist and antagonist who often have an ultimate face-off during the climax of the story.

The Coming of Age Quest

Many fantasy stories feature a protagonist who is on a quest to find out who he or she really is after making a shocking discovery—such as, he was adopted at birth, or she has a special ability. This goal can serve as the main plot or as a sub-plot. For example, the main story goal in Harry Potter was a good versus evil quest with a coming of age basis in the first book. Coming of age goals in fantasy open doors for conflicts with morality, good versus evil, psychological growth, and with society's values. There is often a heavy amount of magic involved with fantasy coming of age stories.

Save the Village

A goal of saving the village or townsfolk is a classic story goal in fantasy literature. Usually paired with the theme of good versus evil, the protagonist with this goal often finds himself faced with the task of defeating evil while under the pressure of incredibly high stakes–for example, the entire town being in danger.

Survive a Foreign World

In some fantasy stories, the protagonist's goal is to simply survive a foreign world until he or she can get back home. This rings true in stories such as *The Wizard of Oz* and *Alice in Wonderland*. Along the way, the protagonist often befriends the creatures of that world and sometimes runs into a force of evil that he or she must defeat.

Damsel in Distress

Rescuing the damsel in distress story goal for a protagonist is another popular fantasy storyline. The female character in need of rescuing often turns out to be a person of importance, say, a princess or the daughter of a powerful person in the community. The male protagonist, sets off to rescue the female character and often runs into challenging obstacles along the way.

Win a War

Battle is a common event in fantasy, so it would be no surprise to readers if your protagonist's goal was to win a war. The war could be between two races, two lands or any two opposing forces. Sometimes the final confrontation is solely between the protagonist and the antagonist; other times it could be a full-on war with multiple characters on each side. A goal of winning a war often incorporates the good versus evil theme, because the protagonist and antagonist are usually fighting on opposite sides. The war can also be against something less tangible. For example, a whole village could be fighting a deadly disease that threatens to wipe out their entire civilization.

Escape from Danger

Escaping from danger is an adequate story goal in fantasy writing. Usually the protagonist is the one who is in danger and is trying to get away. The danger is often exciting, such as being trapped in a dungeon or trying to escape man-eating lions. You can use anything that will get your readers' adrenaline rushing.

Family Values

A very powerful story goal for a character in a fantasy story can be to find out about themselves through their family. Often, the story focuses on a protagonist who knows nothing or little about her family and has a strong craving to find out. Along the way, the protagonist starts to learn things about his or her family and discovers things that are surprising, shocking or sad. In the end, the pursuit usually affects the protagonist, whether by choosing the opposite path or by upholding the family legacy.

Clearing a Name

One story goal option for your protagonist can be to clear his or her name after a betrayal. When a character needs to clear his or her name, a trap has usually been set up by an antagonist. The protagonist aims to bring justice to the real villain. The plot twist in a storyline like this usually consists of a discovery that will help prove his innocence.

Overcome a Weakness

Another fantasy goal option is to have your protagonist overcome a weakness. Since the term "overcome a weakness" is so vague, you can be quite creative here and give your protagonist any weakness you want. For example, your protagonist could be training to become a warrior, learning how to use their magic or special abilities for positive things, or trying to achieve redemption for a failed mission.

A Struggle over a Magical Item

The struggle over a magical item can make for an impressive story goal in fantasy. This story goal can be found in classics such as *The Lord of the Rings,* where the struggle is over the ring, and in *The Wizard of Oz*, where the struggle is over the ruby slippers. In a storyline like this, it is usually up to the protagonist to keep the magical item out of the wrong hands.

Courage, Friendship and Honor

Courage, friendship and honor are more like a theme than a story goal but when mixed together, it can create a powerful storyline. Part of the story goal can be for your protagonist to build these three factors while achieving the bigger part of their goal, such as overcoming a weakness or saving the village.

Chapter 5: Fantasy Frameworks

Writing a fantasy book can be overwhelming, especially if it's your first time. Luckily, you can pretty easily get a handle on the big picture and maintain continuity across hundreds of pages–using outlines. I recommend that you outline, not just the story itself but each major aspect: the plot, your characters, the chapters, and scenes within those chapters. With these aspects outlined, you are able to easily access and reference the most important parts of your story.

While some writers depend heavily upon outlining to get them through the writing process, others hate outlines and firmly resist their use. Managing via outlines is a personal preference, but I think you can benefit from this discipline, especially in the beginning. Don't begrudge yourself the time it takes; the process of outlining multiple aspects of your story will actually help ensure you don't miss important details. By the time you have completed your outlines, you will be fully prepared to start the actual writing.

The best way to approach outlining is with an open, flexible mind. Outlines can feel rigid, but they're not intended to trap or confine you–their purpose is to give you a big-picture view of your story; in that way, they can actually reduce your stress. Think of an outline as a roadmap; it's meant to guide you along a specific route, but that does not mean you are forbidden from taking side trips along the way. I like outlines because they help me test how far I can develop my ideas. If I outline an idea and see that I can take it really deep, then I know it's worth developing further. If I can't really flesh out an idea, then I know not to waste my time on it. Outlines can help prevent dead-ends in your plot as well as ensuring consistency in your writing.

The Elevator Pitch

I like to start out my outline by defining the storyline in one to three sentences. Pretend you're crafting an elevator pitch about your book. It should be short but packed with enough interesting details to stop people in their tracks.

First, describe your protagonist, either by name (if a well-known person) or by personality. Unless your protagonist is a household word, you should stick to generic terms in your storyline sentence. For example, if you had a protagonist named Stanley who was a loner, you would omit the name and just describe him as a loner. However, if your first book was a hit and you are now building a whole series around Stanley, by all means capitalize on the name recognition and thereby connect your readers to this new release.

Include:

- The situation at the beginning of the story and your protagonist's goal

- The first plot twist or obstacle and the conflict that follows

- A mention of the antagonist

Here is an example of a storyline:

When a depressed prince (the protagonist) finally finds the woman of his dreams (the current situation), he vows to become her husband (the goal). But when this girl (the antagonist) turns out to be a commoner (the first plot twist or obstacle), the prince refuses to let go, stopping at nothing–not even the risk of losing his throne–to get her (the conflict).

The Synopsis

After the summary, you will write your book's **synopsis.** A synopsis is a brief sketch of your storyline. You should always write your synopsis in the third person and using the present tense. Start with your plot outline, then expand upon it to create a story synopsis in a maximum of two pages. Touch on each plot twist and include major story events.

The first step in writing a synopsis is to flesh out the beginning of your story. Keep in mind that this will be the first thing a prospective publisher will see. It also determines whether a reader will keep reading, so skillfully insert your story hook and provide as much vivid action as possible. Highlight the first plot twist your protagonist encounters.

Next, summarize the middle of your story, highlighting the second and third plot twists. Toward the end of this section, you will summarize the events or issues that lead your characters toward their final confrontation.

Finally, sketch out the climax of the tale by describing its final conflict and showing briefly whether or not your protagonist achieves the desired objective. A solid synopsis will stand on its own, without needing further details. I encourage you to test your synopsis by asking someone who knows nothing about your story to read it and give you some feedback.

The Scene List

Another way to lay out your story is with a **scene list**. A scene list can provide a complete overview of your book in just a few pages, thus serving as a useful organizational tool. Scene lists make it easier to edit your book once you've finished. They assist you in identifying and deleting unnecessary scenes and can help you know exactly where is the best place to insert anything essential that has been overlooked.

To make a scene list, create a spreadsheet or a table with six columns. Label these columns "Scene Name," "Characters," "Point of View," "Location," "Summary," and

"Moves Plot Forward?" then, starting with the first row and fill in the information for the first scene. In the first column, give your scene a name or other identifier. Moving to the right, list each character that appears in the scene, followed by whose point of view is used, and the location of the scene. Then write a couple of sentences briefly summarizing how the scene progresses and write "Yes" or "No," based on whether or not the scene moves the plot forward. If it does not, then you may be able to omit the scene.

Each scene you write should be interrelated with the others and look to at least move toward answering the reader's questions and further development of the major themes of your book. For example, if you plan a scene in which your protagonist discovers he has a child he didn't know about, then you're going to need to set up the scene so your readers will say, "That makes sense." In this scenario, I would write an earlier scene where your protagonist and a respective character have a meeting where a secret could be revealed, but an argument breaks out and the secret is never told.

Some writers use flowcharts to portray the progression of their story. This involves using boxes to show movement from the exposition, to the rising action, on to the climax, and then to the resolution of your story. Boxes representing the development of themes usually run beneath the story flow.

The ending of your book requires special attention. Your ending will be your last contact with the reader; in it you have one final opportunity to leave a lasting impression. Break down your ending into several scenes that build suspense and lead to a strong and memorable resolution. Sometimes I am so strongly aware of how I want to end a book that I'll write the ending first; then I will deconstruct the story backwards. This reverse-order process enables me to space out the prerequisite details across previous scenes, giving various levels of obscure hints as to what is to come.

If later I find that the ending just doesn't work, I can always change it. Never think your work is wasted when you need to delete whole sections. Writing is a process, usually a process of trial and error. Every step you take is necessary, even if it looks like you are wasting whole chapters full of hard work. Each idea you scrap helps eliminate the unnecessary so that you can discover the best path for your story. Some books are like that. They will demand to go places you did not foresee. No worry; you can always rewrite as needed. If you truly have no idea what kind of ending to write, set your work aside for a few days. When you come back to it, first read through everything you have written, looking for leads you can pursue that might take you to a satisfying ending. Often, just backing away briefly will add enough objectivity to clarify where your story wants to take you.

The Character List

In Chapter three we talked about making a character list to help stay organized. We discussed important questions *about* your character but omitted the character description itself.

You can describe your character throughout the story itself because that helps give your readers a mental picture but during the outlining process, I recommend making a very detailed description. Consider everything, including details about body language, facial features, expression, and thought processes. Put yourself in your character's shoes and try to describe him from that point of view. I like to have one master document per story with each character listed on a separate page. Then I use an entire page to create an individual's profile. Sometimes I'll go really crazy and even decide where they go to school or where they work. Those details can unlock storylines like you'd never believe.

Help! I'm Stuck!

Finally, I love the outlining process because sometimes it helps me overcome writer's block. I'll be honest; if I have an idea, I'll often skip the outlining process and jump straight into sporadic writing and only return to the outline when I've run up against a wall in my writing. As I said earlier, I believe the outlining process can be very inspiring and creative. With almost every story I've written, I've turned to outlining, at least eventually.

For example, writing a synopsis often helps me brainstorm ideas where the story goes to next. I might have my story written up the first plot point but then I'll be left clueless once I'm at the midpoint. At the first plot point, I can start asking myself, "Well what if..." and see if I can come up with a good midpoint scenario. I try to ask myself what my readers would and would not expect and pick the more exciting route (usually what they wouldn't expect). If I really cannot pick something, sometimes I'll invent a new character and find a way to work him or her into the tale.

The outlining process also enables me to backtrack. If I'm writing a scene list and come across a scene that I think is boring, the outlining process allows me to go back and rework it rather than just scrapping it altogether. It also enables me to take a break from writing one scene and jump to another if I can't figure out where to take it.

Some other things you can do to help beat writers' block are to do some research for inspiration or experiment with switching point of view. Research sounds awful but sometimes it can be really fun! For example, I thought about writing a story about gangs, but I have no knowledge of gangs or how they work, so I read a memoir about gangs to get a better idea. Switching the point of view in a scene is more like a creative writing activity to help you gain a more rounded view of your story and characters.

Finally, I've always found that simply taking a break helps me. Sitting at a computer for long hours can be draining. I know that I usually get tired and hungry, so I'll go grab a bite to eat, do something fun for a little bit (maybe listen to music or watch a show), just get my eyes away from the screen and I'll usually come back feeling refreshed. I also always go back over the parts of the story I wrote as my tiredness was setting in because eight out of ten times I find that's where I start rushing and slacking off.

Chapter 6: Writing Tips and Strategies

Keep Details Consistent

Keeping your details consistent in a fantasy story is very important for gaining the trust of your readers and for writing a story that makes sense. Since fantasy often incorporates creative details, such as magic or races made up by you, it burdens you with more responsibility, as you work to make sure that your story is consistent and organized. For example, if only one race of characters in your story can use magic, you wouldn't want to write a scene where both races are utilizing magic. Writers often work long hours, so it is easy to forget those types of details. That's only one reason to proofread your story several times and to maintain a spreadsheet listing all the skills of each character.

Consider Language

The language of your story can set the tone and help your readers understand when and/or where the story is taking place. For example, if you write a sentence in your story that describes the town hall as "Ye Old Town Hall," then your readers can easily guess that the story is set in medieval times. Using language that matches the specifics of your book can also enhance the readers' experiences by making them feel they are inside the story.

Create an Exciting Cover

"Don't judge a book by its cover," is a popular phrase but, unfortunately, that rule doesn't usually apply in book sales. Think back to the last time you were in a book store and were browsing books to buy. Did you immediately pick one up because the cover looked exciting to you? Personally, I am drawn to books either because I've heard the title before or because of what's on the cover. Boring, bland covers don't sell well, especially in fantasy. If you are going to be writing a fantasy novel that you would like to see published or self-published, you're going to also need to come up with a fantastic cover.

When designing a cover, the most important factor to consider is this: does the artwork reflect the tone and voice of your novel? Let's consider a few real-life examples to demonstrate this. A quick Google search for "The Hobbit" yields several different covers but they all reflect the spirit of the story. Most of the results show a scenic cover with mountains, trees and a pathway, which makes sense if you know the premise of the book. Another good example is the cover for the first Harry Potter book. It depicts a young boy with a cape, playing a wizard's sport in a wizard-like setting; it immediately gives the reader an idea of about the main aspects of the book.

If you are not a respectable graphic artist, I would strongly recommend outsourcing your cover art. In the past, I've tried to provide my own covers, but I have found they don't look very appetizing when set next to professionally designed covers. You can easily find an artist on talent websites such as www.Fiverr.com, who will create a quality book cover for you, often for less than $20 and as little as $5. Whether hiring a cover artist or doing the work yourself, you need to decide the dimensions, or size, of your book before you can design its cover. If self-publishing, your publisher will help you decide this. Many publishing websites have downloadable cover templates that will help guide you, both in selecting a book size and in designing your cover. Finally, a reminder: never use another artist's work without permission.

Crafting Fight Scenes

Fighting or combat scenes are very common in fantasy stories and are often part of the struggle between good and evil. Since battle scenes are full of action, it is important to know how to strategically write them for optimal visualization. Unlike the movies, where the audience can see the two characters physically fighting right on the screen, reading it requires the audience to create their own picture. Your job, as the writer, is to help them build that experience as vividly as possible.

First, make your fight scenes realistic and consistent with the other details of your story. For example, if your story is set in medieval times, your characters can't pull out automatic weapons on each other, unless of course, they are time travelers. If your weapons and combat techniques do not match the setting and era, your readers may start questioning your abilities as a writer. Do your homework and make sure that your fight scenes make sense.

One benefit of writing a fight scene as opposed to watching it on a screen is that you can take advantage of time. In a movie, the audience mostly just gets to see the action but in a book, the audience can also see the thoughts and feelings of the characters involved. This opens a door for building suspense and developing your character as you describe his inner world. Although this may extend a fighting scene, if done right, it can be a powerful technique for driving your plot. If done correctly, your reader won't even notice the time difference.

Another extremely important factor to remember in writing fight scenes: avoid passive voice at all costs! Fight scenes are supposed to be full of fast-paced action; the best way to demonstrate that is to directly show who or what is performing an action. Let's look at two sentences and determine which one sounds better:

"Ash quickly swung the war hammer into Wiley's head."

"The war hammer was quickly swung into Wiley's head."

The first sentence puts your readers in the heat of the moment while the second, the passive sentence makes it sound as if your readers are hearing about something that happened in the past. A good way to identify passive voice in your writing is to ask yourself, "*Who* is performing this action?" If the sentence identifies the "who," then you're good. If it doesn't, rewrite your battle scene, making your characters do the fighting, not their weapons!

Give Your Book a Glossary

If your fantasy book is filled with creative words or languages, I recommend you include a glossary at the back of your book. The more complex your story, the more help your readers will need to understand your world. A glossary allows your audience to easily reference words they don't know or figure out how to pronounce strange-sounding names. Try to keep your glossary short and simple; your readers want your book for the story, not the references. However, a glossary can heighten your readers' experience and help them become familiarized with your writing.

Establish Your Protagonist or Hero Right Away

Many fantasy stories include a broad array of characters, so chances are that yours will, too. To avoid confusion, I advise you establish your protagonist, or hero, early. You don't want to confuse your readers by dropping in a bunch of characters without cluing them in as to who are most important. Don't be obvious about it, by stating "This is Thrall, the hero of the story." Use the "show, don't tell" rule to help your readers understand who the hero is, through point of view and writing greater detail into your main character from the start.

Give Your Characters Weaknesses

It would make sense to have incredibly powerful characters in a fantasy story but you mustn't forget that powerful characters should have weaknesses, too. If you have a character that is all power and has no flaws, there won't be any conflict and your readers will likely lose interest fast. Give your characters, even the most powerful ones, weaknesses. Weaknesses are often the window of opportunity for your protagonist's victory.

Be Open to Feedback

Fantasy writing can be a challenging, time-consuming task that requires practice to master. Whether you're a first-time writer or a seasoned pro, you can't expect to sit down and write an amazing story on the first try. It has taken some writer's years to perfect their stories from the time they first think of the idea to the time they actually finish writing. If you open your mind to feedback and critique, your chances of coming up with an impressive final draft will be greater.

There are many free resources and communities online where experienced writers will give you feedback on your writing. Many writers find themselves closed-minded to this technique because, after all, who likes having their creative works picked apart? It can sting, especially the first few times, but it can be very helpful. If you don't want to post your works online, an alternative option is to ask a creative writing teacher or even a friend who enjoys reading fantasy for his or her opinion.

Write with Heart

Put your heart into whatever you're writing. Write about what you're truly thinking about deep in your heart. Stories that are written straight from the heart often have a natural flow that captures the readers' attention. Passionate writing rarely sounds forced and if you've been writing for a while, your passion can make your story sound even more wonderful.

Don't Quit Until You Finish

Writing a story is hard work and it can be tempting to give up halfway through. When I wrote my first book, I nearly gave up after six months, thinking I would never finish; then something deep within told me to keep going. I'm glad I persevered, because before long, I had self-published my first book! It may seem hard, but if you just keep working your way through the tough spots, the final result will feel great. Don't rush yourself. It only takes some writers a few months to write a book, where it can take others years. Work at your own pace. One thing I have learned is to never rush. Sometimes I think I rushed my first book; now I wonder what would be the end product if I had taken it slower.

Edit Well

Editing your book is another top priority in the world of writing. Editing is what allows you to go over your first and subsequent drafts, perfecting them for your readers. Many writers try to edit as they go along. However, that method can distract from the main purpose of the first draft, which is to capture your raw thoughts before they fly away. I think that editing is best saved until after the first draft of your book is completed. I know quite a few writers who are tempted to go back and edit their work after writing a paragraph or a chapter, but I think premature editing interrupts the flow of my true words.

Subplots

A subplot is an additional plot in your story, structured in the same way as the main plot, but on a smaller scale. Writers generally use subplots to strengthen the main plot. Subplots should be concluded before the actual conclusion of your story. They can involve your protagonist or a minor character. For example: A king has to execute a murderer for the good of his kingdom (main plot) while also dealing with his wife, the Queen, who is causing marriage problems (subplot). Not every story needs a subplot, but it can definitely be helpful in turning a shorter story into a longer one. Subplots can also add variety to your story and help keep your readers interested and guessing.

Since adding subplots to your story can be complex, I recommend treating each subplot as a separate short story, then editing it into the main story during the editing process. This is where a scene list comes in handy, because you can easily give yourself an overview of each plot and organize each one as needed. Build each subplot as strong and as solid as if it were your main plot; otherwise it will weaken, rather than strengthen, your story.

Here are a few more **YouTube** resources that offer additional fantasy writing tips and strategies:

- Fantasy Writing Tips by ShadeVlog

- Why is Fantasy Writing So Hard by Grauwelt

- How to Make a Fantasy Novel Outline by Grauwelt

Chapter 7: Fantasy Idea-Drivers

In order to write fantasy, you will need an idea. If you're already a writer, I bet somebody has asked you where your idea came from. Ideas are strange things. Sometimes they hit a writer like an eighteen-wheeler out of nowhere; other times finding one is more like pulling teeth! I know many writers who base their stories off real life events and then give them a twist. The truth is, in most cases, coming up with your big idea is a process. I mentioned earlier that sometimes I get inspired by watching movies or playing video games. It can be different for everyone, but there are a few universal strategies you can use to get started. In this chapter, you will discover how you can generate ideas and possibly start writing the world's next best-seller.

For those who tend to have ideas hit them out of nowhere, I recommend keeping a small notepad with you so you can write the ideas down as they come. Your idea may be so incredible that you think you won't forget it, but it's easy to forget even incredible ideas when you've got a lot going on all around.

When I was younger, I used to have wild dreams that often became the basis for my stories. As an adult, I now keep a dream journal next to my bed with a pen so I can write about dreams I remember as soon as I wake up, before I forget them in the busy rush of the day. You can use almost any dream or dream fragment as a jumping off point. Just start writing and see if you can develop some new ideas from there. You might not get a whole story idea from a dream, or you might glean a character or an idea for a plot twist. The protagonist for my friend's first self-published book came to her in a dream.

Another way to generate ideas is to observe something and then ask why. For example, "Why is that big brick building abandoned?" "Why is it sitting in the middle of a small residential neighborhood?" Perhaps the building was once used as a secret-agent hideout and they built it in the middle of a residential neighborhood thinking that nobody would expect to find secret agents there. As with of the use of the female construction worker, allow your creativity free rein and see what emerges.

Here are a few common fantasy tools you can use to stimulate creative ideas for your story:

Elves

Elves are human-like creatures that often have a positive connection with nature and have been inspired by mythology, folklore and Victorian literature. Stereotypical elves have long, pointed ears, are wise, immortal and have magical abilities. Elves are good to include in stories that are set in ancient times, as they tend to be one of the longest living races around. Many fantasy tales feature elves as the primary race.

Orcs

Orcs are well-known fantasy creatures closely related to goblins but can physically act nearly the same as humans. The earliest written record of orcs appears in sixteenth century literature. Stereotypical orcs have a human stature but are ugly, with pig-like facial features and an aggressive nature. The color of their skin can vary but is traditionally green or black. J.R.R. Tolkien was the first author to make orcs popular in our day, via *The Lord of the Rings*. Orcs have subsequently made appearances in other fantasy stories and in video games.

Dragons

Dragons are legendary creatures derived from the mythologies of multiple cultures. The Greek word for dragon is literally translated "water snake" or "serpent of huge size." Various legends, believed even today, hold that parts of a dragon, such as dragon blood, can be either beneficial or dangerous. Dragons usually breathe fire from their nose and are violent, although some stories and movies depict them as friendly and gentle. Their body is often large, with wings and scales for skin. When a violent dragon appears in a fantasy tale, you will usually find a corresponding character whose goal is to slay the dragon. Dragons can be used to symbolize spirituality and can also represent the power of nature.

Dwarves

Dwarves are short, ugly, and wise creatures who are known to live in the mountains or underground and perform laborious work such as mining, making crafts, and doing blacksmith work. Dwarves have been found in literature as early as Norse mythology. They can be either friendly or violent. Today dwarves are often evident in pop culture works and fantasy games such as Dungeons and Dragons.

Wizards

A wizard, also known as a magician, is a being who uses magic that stems from a supernatural ability. In fantasy, wizards often possess their magical abilities through talent, study or inheritance. Wizards classically appear as the "wise old man" stereotype, but as literature has expanded, it has become acceptable for wizards to be of any age. Stereotypical wizards have flowing white beards and wear long robes decorated with stars and moons, along with matching pointed hats. Wizards often play a teaching or mentoring role; some can be absent-minded or clumsy, like a professor who is so preoccupied with research he can hardly tie his shoes. Wizards may be good or evil. They usually carry an accessory such as a staff, a book, a wand or a crystal ball.

Magic

A fantasy book can contain magic, with or without wizards. As the writer, you can assign magic abilities to any of your characters. There are a variety of characters who can perform magic, such as enchanters, sorcerers and witches. Magic has been used as a plot device in many books since the time of Homer. Writing about magic can be as detailed or as basic as you want. However, if you do choose to incorporate magic into your story, always give it some limits; otherwise, there will be no room for building conflict.

Royalty

Fantasy stories often revolve around kingdoms that are run by royal families. In a kingdom, there is usually a King, a Queen and a son or daughter who serves as the Prince or Princess and future ruler of the kingdom. Fantasy stories featuring kingdoms often incorporate the good versus evil theme, where some sort of curse or enemy takes hold of the kingdom. The king, or another heroic character, sets off the fight the evil force and bring solace back to the kingdom once and for all. These types of stories also feature characters such as knights, butlers, royal political powers, and jokers.

Magical Items

Including magical items in your fantasy story can serve as a powerful plot device, because two opposing forces usually fight over the magic item, creating conflict without hardly trying. For example, consider the conflict surrounding the ring in *The Lord of the Rings* and the ruby slippers in *The Wizard of Oz*. These magical items of interest always have one or more powerful abilities that make the stakes high and add tension to the story, just so your readers don't get bored.

Psychic Abilities

Psychics are paranormal characters who possess extrasensory abilities and often appear in science fiction and fantasy stories. Your fantasy story can be about psychic abilities, no matter what era it is set in, because psychics have been around from ancient times. Any type of character can have psychic abilities, ranging from humans to ghosts. Including a character with psychic abilities in your fantasy story is one way to create suspense and build tension.

Giants

Giants are a race of beings known from ancient times, which are defined by their size, their powerful strength and their visible aggression. Giants tend to be human or near-human. Some cultures believe that giants are buried under land masses and cause earthquakes and volcanic eruptions. There are many ancient stories about giants–probably most famously in *The Odyssey*. Greek mythology links giants to Olympian Gods such as Gaia and Uranus. Although giants have a reputation for being violent, some fantasy stories have depicted them as gentle and friendly, such as Hagrid in *Harry Potter*.

Ghosts/Spirits

Dating back to ancient mythology and found in the folklore of multiple cultures, ghosts or spirits are considered to be the souls of former living beings that can appear visibly to those who are still living. The appearance of ghosts has been described in a variety of forms: transparent, lifelike, orbs of energy, gasses, completely invisible, and fully lifelike. Ghosts usually haunt a specific place or object, hanging around it to scare or interact with humans. They sometimes appear in the form of stationary objects such as a ship or a train. They can also appear in the form of animals. Ghosts often play important roles in fantasy fiction, serving as antagonists, mentors, guardians, and even sometimes, protagonists.

Weather

The weather is another item that can help shape your fantasy story. Weather can be a natural phenomenon, or it may be linked to a greater force, such as an evil or benevolent being. The storyline in the video game *Tomba* focuses on a curse set upon the land by a group of evil pigs. The curse specifically messes up the weather and geography of the land, but once the protagonist of the story starts to kill off the pigs, the curse is broken and the land goes back to normal.

Fairies

Fairies are a popular focus of fantasy stories. Fairies originated in European and Celtic folklore as mythical people or supernatural spirits. While modern media often depict fairies as small, human-like creatures, often with wings similar to dragonflies', older folk tales often depict them as tall, angelic creatures. Fairies also tend to possess magical powers, such as being able to heal or grant wishes. In some cases, fairies can actually be demons in hiding.

Vampires

Originating with 18th century folklore, vampires are mythical creatures famous for feeding on the blood of other lifeforms. Literature, such as Bram Stoker's *Dracula,* made vampires a popular character in fiction. Vampires became a growing superstition in Europe; at one point people actually began to accuse others of being vampires, in some cases killing them with a stake through the heart, as that was considered the only way to make a vampire remain dead. These days, the majority of people believe that vampires are just fictional creatures who appear in fantasy stories.

The description of a vampire varies by culture, ranging from a pale human-like creature with black hair and red eyes to a bloated being with purple skin, who wears a shroud. Both Slavic and Chinese folklore suggest that a human body turns into a vampire when jumped over by an animal. Russian folklore suggests that vampires are those who were originally witches. According to most folktales, only a specific apotropaic, such as garlic, can be used to ward them off. Vampires are traditionally viewed as evil but modern media, such as the *Twilight* series has challenged that belief.

Witches

Witches are traditional fixtures of fantasy stories. They are well-known from fairy tales, such as *Hansel and Gretel*, and are often evil, although this can also go either way, as with most other fantasy character types. According to North American folklore, witches–known as hags–represented a nightmare spirit. Early on, witches were used as a device to scare young children into behaving. Irish and Scottish mythology doesn't depict witches as evil, but connects them to the weather and nature.

Aliens

Aliens are beings believed to come from another planet or location in outer space. While modern science focuses on the debate as to whether aliens really do exist, they can certainly exist in a fantasy story. There have been many fantasy stories about aliens, including *The War of the Worlds* and movies such as *E.T.* In fantasy stories, aliens can either be bad or good. In terms of appearance, aliens tend to be human-like or similar to reptiles or insects. They often have green or gray skin, big heads, and large eyes. Aliens often have supernatural powers, such as telepathy or the ability to fly. In most fantasy stories, the aliens often have a specific reason for coming to Earth, if they visit Earth at all.

Foreign Lands/Worlds

Another option can be to have your fantasy story focus on the world itself, although this usually requires a very unique world created by you. The characters are usually lost or trapped in this world and have to find a way to get back home. For example, Alice stumbles upon a completely different fantasy world in the book *Alice in Wonderland,* as does Dorothy in *The Wizard of Oz.*

Animals

Animals are often a focal point in fantasy stories. They can be minor or major characters. In many cases, animals possess a special power, such as the ability to think or speak like humans. Animals can be common, such as horses or pigs, or they may be legendary, such as Krakens (Japanese sea monsters) or Chakoras (Hindu lunar birds). Although animals often appear in fantasy stories for children, they can play a role in stories for any age.

Swords and Sorcery

Swords and sorcery are exciting ideas to incorporate in heroic fantasy. Often, the protagonist is a sword-fighting hero who encounters violent conflicts while fighting a personal battle. Romance, magic, and the supernatural are also frequent visitors to stories about swords and sorcery. While as ancient as the Arthurian legend, the category of swords and sorcery was popularized in 1961 by Michael Moorcock. Swords and sorcery stories are largely influenced by both history and mythology.

Dungeons

Dungeons can serve as a magnificent focal point for your story. Dungeons are miserable subterranean prisons, often situated beneath a castle, where prisoners encounter painful torture and indefinite imprisonment. If you include dungeons in your story, your characters can be trapped in them while trying to escape, or they can imprison additional characters, holding them for later use in your tale.

Treasures

Treasures are another exciting plot device in fantasy stories. Who doesn't desire treasure? Treasures can be anything valuable to a character. It can be a chest filled with diamonds and gold or it could be a set of important family heirlooms or anything in between, as long as it is of value to the characters in the story. When there is a treasure at the center of a story, the protagonist and the antagonist are usually in a race to see who can get the treasure first.

Apocalypses

Apocalyptic stories have become increasingly popular in the last few years. An apocalypse literally means "the disclosure of knowledge" in Greek and the term is often connected to tragedies that mark the end of the world. In the Bible, the apocalyptic book entitled "Revelation" describes both the end of the world as we know it and the final victory of good over evil. An apocalypse in a fantasy story could mean a cataclysmic natural disaster within a world or its ultimate destruction by an evil force. When an apocalypse occurs, the protagonist often receives a warning revelation of sorts through a dream, a messenger—angelic, wizardly or otherwise—or through an accidental discovery.

Chapter 8: Powerful Finales

By now you've probably heard enough about the first-half of your book–how important it is to start out fast, hook your reader, and hold their attention. What about the other half of your book: the ending? An ending is important for two primary reasons: It will influence whether readers buy another book by you and it will leave your reader with some sort of response to the story question. Writing a fantasy story can be difficult and tiring, but once you've come to the end, you don't want to stop too early. If you quit before mastering the ending, all of your hard work may fly right out the door! In this chapter, you will learn how to pen a compelling ending that can make your readers eager to get their hands on your next book.

Rule #1: Reflect Your Theme in the Ending

Does the conclusion of your book reflect on its theme? Readers usually like to revisit the theme at the end. For example, if your protagonist is able to defeat the antagonist through unconditional love, it fulfills the theme of "love triumphs over evil."

Rule #2: Bask In the Pleasure

By all means, you're allowed to have a happy ending. In fact, I encourage you to have a happy ending. But don't dump the ending on your readers suddenly, with no warning, or you will leave them hanging in the air. Your job is to bring them to a soft landing back on planet Earth. Lead up to your happy ending with details that foreshadow the ending, but don't give it completely away until the last moment. Don't just say "Harry's family lived happily ever after." That can be very unsatisfying to your audience. If you've written dynamic characters, your readers will need some time to gently disengage their emotions. They need to feel things winding down. As you end your story, account for what happens to each major character. Then, give your readers a few moments to wallow in the warmth of a wonderful ending before they close the book.

Rule #3: Write a Satisfying Surprise Ending

Surprise endings are one way to get an impressive shock out of your readers. However, you must write them using appropriate strategies. Surprise endings are most satisfying when the reader isn't able to predict them, but to be successful, you will need to hint that something mysterious is on the way. We call this foreshadowing and you can sprinkle elements throughout your book. Drop hints so that in the end, your reader can say "Oh, *that's* why the author said that, back there," and be content. One thing I've learned over years of writing is that if you're going to create a huge shock at the end of your book, make it a satisfying shock. If you just randomly throw in something that has nothing to do with the story or its theme, your readers will not be satisfied. The best surprise endings provide unexpected resolutions to multiple plot lines, simultaneously.

Rule #4: Tie Up Loose Ends

Avoid leaving your reader hanging unless, of course, your book is part of a series, in which it's okay to leave some issues unresolved. However, ensure that your reader can easily identify your book as part of a series. Even a simple "To Be Continued" disclaimer at the end will enable your readers to confirm that there's more to come. Otherwise, they may feel cheated and used, and decide they have wasted their money. This is especially important when writing fantasy, because many writers like to turn fantasy books into series. The main reason your readers persevere to the end of your tale is to see whether or not your protagonist reaches his goal. If you don't clarify whether or not that occurs, your readers will probably be quite disappointed; they may even avoid your future books. Readers want to see the result of your protagonist's growth at the end of your story. Show how he has become a better or person or how he has grown internally. Leave them feeling that at least the primary question in your story has been resolved completely.

Rule #5: Write Unhappy Endings Carefully

Happy, positive endings are usually the norm for fiction stories, but some authors go the other direction to pen negative endings. Negative endings *can* work, but they require careful attention and preparation. If not well designed, your readers may find an unhappy ending unrealistic and feel cheated out of an experience they've been anticipating over hours of reading.

Unhappy endings tend to require an amount of justification. If your protagonist dies unexpectedly in the end, your readers might have trouble accepting your ending. However, if they already knew he was suffering from a disease, or if he died as a hero in the process of saving the townspeople, they will likely find the ending sad, but justified. Clue your readers into the risks your protagonist is facing well before the story ends.

If an unhappy ending just hits out of nowhere or proves unnecessary, your chances of reader satisfaction are split. Some readers absolutely love endings that take them by total surprise and make them think, but other readers will trash your book for it. If you're going to have an unhappy ending, try to drop hints throughout your book so your readers aren't strongly expecting something different.

Rule#6: On Writing Cliffhangers

Cliffhangers are useful in priming your readers to want more, ensuring a ready-made audience for the next installment in your book series. Your reading public will want to know what happens next, although it can be frustrating for them to have to wait until the next volume is released. A well-written cliffhanger at the end of an amazing story can leave readers talking about it up until the next installment comes out. Here's how to write an amazing cliffhanger:

Although cliffhangers can be occasionally useful at the end of a chapter to hook your readers into not stopping, it is important that you save your strongest cliffhanger for the end of your book. Readers will have no place else to go after expecting a conclusion, so this is good way to insert additional shock factor. Save the best cliffhanger, the one that will make readers go crazy, for last. Make it quick and sudden. Don't let your readers see it coming. Then, at the start of the next installment, make it a point to immediately address the previous cliffhanger. Remember, your readers have been waiting a long time to get their questions answered. If you don't provide an answer right away, you risk losing their interest and their readership for books you release in the future.

Not sure how to write a cliffhanger? Here is a strategy to try. First, re-read an example of a cliffhanger from a favorite book, watching how the author set it up. Do this with several stories until you have reverse-engineered enough cliffhangers that you can see how they were put together. Next, think of a cliffhanger you can use in your book and carefully weave it into your story. Since you already know what will happen, ask a friend or family member to read your final chapter and see how well the cliffhanger works for them.

A Final Note on Endings

You can always write your ending first. This is usually how I write. If I have a strong idea, I tend to know how I want the story to end, so I write my ending first to capture my ideas in their rawest state. I find that if I write the ending first, it enables me to better set up my story as I write it through. However, sometimes I'm not sure exactly how I want the story to end. In that case, I will start writing and trust that the ending will make itself known later. If you write your ending first, remember you can always go back and change it as needed. Nothing is set in concrete until your book is in print.

Conclusion

I hope this book was able to help you to discover how to plan, set up, and write amazing fantasy stories.

Your next step is to develop an idea and then start planning out your first book. One way to get started is to brainstorm several different routes for your idea to take, and then start to piece it together using an outline. Once you've developed an outline you really like, you can use it as a guide to start fleshing out your book.

I suggest you keep your outline in a separate document. Start a blank page and label different sections for your storyline, the story goal, and the story question. List your protagonists, antagonists, and minor characters. Then state the conflict, the theme, and your story's genre. I also find it useful to outline the plot twists within a three-act structure. I then begin to fill in the blanks, making changes until I have come up with a solid plot I like.

I recommend writing a synopsis, so you will have a detailed but overall picture of where your story will go. At this point, you should be able to envision your fantasy world peopled with your protagonist, antagonist and all the exciting creatures and magical fantastic elements you have chosen.

Then write. Write your little heart out, following the story wherever it leads you. Persist until you have a first draft, then edit the dickens out of it, welcoming skilled criticism along the way, until you have the best fantasy story you can make!

Sneak Preview of The Angel's Blessing

Chapter 1 The Day of the White Rook

My Master did not become the great Warrior Shaman of peace because he was born with the blessings of the gods. He did not rise to his exalted place in the history of our worlds by the chance of ancestry, nor was he a child of fortune. He had no advantage other than his cunning, and he had no blessing other than that given to him by his grandfather. And that blessing was herb-lore.

My master was conceived and born in violence.

His mother was a young beauty who was ravaged by the invading Veylus pirates when our beloved city of Barnacle Atoll was overrun. When her time to give birth came, she held the newborn infant to her breast, the scrawny infant seeking to suckle a tit. But the nipple that the child found was cold and so he turned to his grandfather's thumb instead, and that thumb was hard and calloused and yet rich with the taste of mother-earth and her herbs. And so in his first suckle of life, the babe that was to be known simply as Kell, tasted the roots of us all.

Kell spent his youngest years under the domination of the brigands, and he quickly learned stealth and cunning as a way of life. In time, the Veylus were ousted by the armada of Queen Anastasias, and while her liberation was near devastation, the people of the Barnacles were once again free. With that freedom came years of reconstruction and tribute to the Queen, but that was far better than the pirates.

In that time Kell grew up as boys will. He was astounded with the world. His grandfather had a bountiful garden, and in there Kell saw crawlers and wigglers and flyers of all sorts. As a toddler, he tasted them and found them much crunchier than the wiggly ones of the root cellar. His grandfather often looked at him and sighed as adults will. But despite his odd tastes, he grew up healthy and strong.

Their small island of Dunsil wasn't on many sea-routes, but he and his grandfather were often visited by passing ships looking for a remedy to help a wounded or sick crewman. Often a boatful of sailors would come ashore and seek one of grandfather's special elixirs, and then ask of the ways with which to work the earth's gift. His grandfather never refused anyone in need -- for a fair price. Over the years, the legends grew of his incredible remedies. It was an ideal childhood and Kell was very happy.

Until the day that the Dorimans engulfed their island.

They were a gang of thugs with ships. Their fleet was small and fast and they would prey on defenseless lands, not to conquer, but to plunder and destroy. And before the Queen's forces could come to aid, they would sail away into the night's fog only to reappear in some other land, rough-handed and demanding. They wore no uniforms, and in their motley gear Kell saw them as something to be afraid of. He was a teenager at the time and the Dorimans saw him as a value to their number. And so at his grandfather's urging, he drew on all his cunning and he ran away.

He ran across the crest of the island and to the common ground where others were also gathering and afraid. Understanding his plight, the elders brought him to a cove with a light boat hidden within. They told him to sail straight to Angove's Cay, which was the home of Wendfala the Witch.

The young witch, seeing my Master's comely and youthful state, took him in and proceeded to teach him the ancient ways. It is said that in those dark hours while our very island writhed beneath the boots of the Dorimans, Wendfala made my Master into a man, and the young boy emerged from her clutches alert, able and with a new sort of strength that radiated off him like an aura.

They say that he emerged from her embraces as a magical paladin who single-handedly rallied the people and sent the Dorimans howling away and afraid. They say that he was the hero who liberated our islands and that the Doriman still fear his name. And they say that when he was done with the Dorimans, the of battle was still upon him, and so he sailed the world in search of glory, wisdom and to inflict Holy

Justice upon the wicked. For years sailors and merchants would land on our island and tell tales of Kell's valor in lands unknown.

That's what they say.

In the years of peace that followed many tales were told and retold, and then told and changed again and again. And in the small confines of the island of Dunsil the simple herbalist's grandchild became a living legend.

He returned to our island the year that I was born, and while many looked at the legendary hero in awe, their real amazement was that the lad looked as if he had never left. It was as though time had not touched him, and when he walked into his grandfather's cottage with his backpack full of magic and treasures, the old man simply looked up and told him that the garden needed tending.

He would say nothing of his adventures, but people would talk. Kell shunned their stories, but he didn't shun their company. He was still young and he had a quick wit at the tavern and loved winning at darts and skittles. The young women all eyed him and so at the festivals and dances he never lacked a partner. His knowledge of herbs and medicines grew as his grandfather taught him all he knew as he waned in years. People came to trust the young man as they did his old grandfather, sometimes more.

In time, the great herbalist finally passed. Every man woman and child on Dunsil stood on the white sands of the island's eastern shore as Kell made ready the last boat. They covered his body in beautiful flower blossoms, in hopes that the sea would pause and delight in the scent and so allow fair winds to carry him to his eternal paradise. Even the witch Wendfala came to give her blessing.

I was just a small boy at the time. I remember my mother urging me, my sisters and my brothers to let go of our flowers. But I was fascinated by the naked old man. He was nothing but old bones wrapped in tan skin at the bottom of a small rustic boat, and yet the blossoms made him seem almost alive.

"Forgive my child Kell," my mother said. "He is –"

"Young," Kell said. "And fascinated."

Then he set his gaze on me and he smiled.

It was not that long after the funeral that I was selected to be Kell's apprentice. I trembled with the honor and surged with excitement.

I had heard all of the grand tales. Indeed, I had been raised in the shadow of those magnificent stories, and when he and my father bartered for my apprenticeship, I thought that the gods themselves had blessed me.

"He's kind of scrawny."

"Yeah," my father said. "He is. But how much bulk do you need to scratch out your herbs?"

Kell frowned.

"Look," my father said. "I have a farm. Farming is a strong man's job. The boy will be better in your hands. I will give you milk, cheese and all the whey you want for four years."

"Seven."

I listened as they haggled over my worth. In the end I went for the price of six years of milk, three of cheeses and all the whey I could carry between the houses until I was seventeen.

It was a good bargain.

Master Kell was a soft-spoken and kindly man. He treated me well and our house wanted for nothing. Along with teaching me herb lore, he also taught me numbers and letters, and while I found numbers valuable in weighing and mixing and figuring out the price to put on a remedy, I never understood why Kell put so much value on writing.

We worked in a daily routine and there were always things to get done or learn. But Kell was a light-hearted soul and we often took the time to play. We would sometimes end a long day frolicking and fishing on one side of Crystal Lake while the women washed their laundry on the other. My master had an eye for the ladies and there were quite a few nights that I spent alone sleeping under the Starlight.

When I came into my teenage years I learned two very important lessons of life. One was girls. When I was young girls were simply giggly playmates, but as I matured I began to see those gigglers grow round, soft and firm, and that made me wonder. And there were odd things about my own body that I didn't understand; strange stirrings and desires. I asked my master about these feelings but he seemed somewhat at a loss, then smiled and assured me that all would be revealed in time.

I wondered about how long that time might be. And then one day a woman named Loleena came calling. She was from the other side of the island and I barely knew her. Kell graciously invited her to sup with us and the woman seemed to take an immediate interest in me. I was flattered that such a fine lady would even recognize my existence, let along talk with me.

The night was cool and getting cooler. Kell excused himself to gather more wood for the fire, but he didn't return till dawn. And that night Loleena helped me understand what it was like to be a man.

Over time I became an expert at herb lore and my master's special elixirs where in high demand, giving me plenty of practice at the craft. When it came time for the harvest festival, I was invited for the first time to join the adults around the big bonfire. There was music and dancing, and everyone cheered when Kell produced a keg of his special brew. The draught was sweet and heady and at first I didn't feel its effects. But then the festival started to feel a lot more happier to me. The dancing was lighter, the music was sweeter, and the young girls seemed prettier. The brew seemed to have the same effect on the girls as well, because they suddenly found me handsome. I did not lack for sweet company all that day and night.

Winters on the Atoll were usually cold and dreary. Work still needed to be done, but the sun would set earlier and earlier and the nights cooped up in the cottage could be wearisome. In those days I was glad to have learned my letters. My master had books on his craft and a boring volume entitled *The List of Leaves* that helped pass the dreary time.

We woke one chill sunny morning to a racket outside. Rooks were calling and crying. We rushed outside to see what was happening and the sky was nearly blotted out by their numbers. It was an amazing sight. Thousands of them were circling overhead. They seemed to be whirling in a vortex that narrowed closer and closer to the center eye, and in that eye I saw a single speck of white.

As we watched the birds became more and more frantic. The center mass of birds began to dip down and then formed into a funnel. I cried out and fell back to shield myself, but when they were only a few hundred feet above us a single rook parted from the myriad, spread its massive wings and began to descend. As it got closer we could see that the rook was as white as snow.

The pearlescent feathers seemed almost to gleam and its beak was like polished marble, but even as its spiny claws touched the sand of the earth the creature transformed. There stood before us a tall, bald man with skin as black as the night that seemed to almost shine blue where the sunlight fell on it. He was hairless from his head to his eyebrows and everywhere else a man should have hair. But what truly astonished me was that there was no manhood. At the place where his thighs met his pelvis there was nothing but smooth dark flesh.

"You are Kell," the man said in a silky, almost liquid voice.

"I am."

And for all of my amazement and growing fear my master was as calm as the sea on a spring morning.

"I am an emissary from Wendfala," he said. "The Witch calls on your pledge."

There was a long pause before my master spoke. The birds above had wheeled out in a huge circle letting the sun shine onto us.

"Why doesn't Wendfala come herself to call on this sacred pledge?" Kell asked in a powerful voice.

"She has been kidnapped," the man-bird said.

"Kidnapped?" Kell bellowed, his hand unconsciously flexing as if to grab his weapon.

"She needs your help. In fact the whole of the Nine domains need your help."

"With what? What is going on?" Kell asked with obvious concern in his voice.

"Wendfala calls for you. It's not for me to judge her choice. I am only a messenger and ask you to hear her plea. I see smoke from your chimney. Can we go inside? It's cold out here without feathers."

"Um, sure. But first tell me, what is your name?" said Kell

"I am Byrinius."

Kell motioned towards his house and as they turned to go inside Byrinius pointed towards me and asked who I was.

"This is Longo Nonan," Kell said. "He is my apprentice."

"Longo," the man said. "Look at me boy. I have no hair and I have nothing where a human male should have something. But can you tell me what else there is about me that is not like you?"

At first I was frightened and my brain refused to work. But it felt as though the two would stare at me until I either flushed or fumbled like a child, or I solved the riddle. I looked. Then I looked again, and then I saw, but the words would not form and so I simply pointed to my belly.

"That's right," Byrinius said laughing long and hard. "I have no naval. I was not born, I was hatched. Kell, the lad is astute. Let him come with us and listen."

My master gave me a strange look, but I went with them and sat quietly in the corner. Kell offered tea but the man refused. He plucked a large ember from the fire, sat at the table, and held the glowing thing in his palm as he spoke.

"Visalth is coming," the man said.

As he spoke, vapors rose from the glowing ember. The smoke grew a little and then began to spin, then gather and spread into a wide sphere, and in the center of the sphere an image began to form. It was the image of a giant skeletal Dragon... A Bone Dragon.

I had heard of such things in stories, and in my youth they were terrifying. The mindless, soulless things would always seek to steal, kill and destroy and they could listen to no reason and had no fear for their own lives.

But these were modern times. Such myths were put away long ago along with frost fairies and trolls.

But that day my eyes had seen a bird transform into the vestige of a man who was now holding a scorching cinder in his hand as if it were a pebble, and the vision that formed in the room made me believe.

The dragon's bones were not like the white bleached things of men I had seen washed up on the beaches. They were deep brown like rotten teeth. It's long skull was swept back, flaring out into nine horns that turned forward like barbed fish-hooks. The hollow orbits were long, narrow and without eyes. It had a look of evil about it. I could not count the many spike-tipped vertebrae of the creature's neck, but the thing could wind and twist like a snake. Its ribs were slender, but what once had been the torso was long. Its fore-limbs grew from a solid breast-plate that looked scarred and beaten, and they were like a man's arms ending in grasping fingers. Its massive hind-legs bent like a deer, but the thighs could have been as thick as a trader ship's mast, and the claws could have crushed our house. The wings that sprouted from its back spread like enormous bird fingers, but between those bones there was no skin, only what looked like remnants of tattered sails or the clinging bits of flesh from creatures undreamed. The tail of the beast was easily as long as the whole creature, and as I watched the dragon fly about in the vision, the bony tail would whip back between the wings to attack like a scorpion.

"Magnificent," Kell said. "Truly a feat of powerful magic."

"Dark magic," Byrinius replied.

We watched the scene as the dragon lay waste to a solid castle set on a hill. The land was unknown to me. It was a lush place with rolling green grass, well cultivated farm land surrounded by walls and then a deep forest. But as we watched, the beast seemed to delight in wreaking ruin on the castle walls and buildings. An army of warriors looked helpless against the skeletal foe. Their arrows and bolts would bounce off the bones or sail through the empty spaces of its ribs. Even the catapults the men managed to muster had little effect, and they were quickly destroyed. When the undead horror had reduced the defenses to rubble it then turned on the army, sweeping men and cavalry away with its deadly tail.

"It seems bent on wanton destruction," Kell said.

"Not so. There is method in its madness. Observe."

I watched with a dull growing terror. When the army had been broken and the warriors were fleeing, men began to march in from the woods. The dragon seemed to suddenly heed some sort of call. It lifted and flew up on wings that were no wings, circling the walled city as the invaders easily took over.

"What are we seeing?" Kell asked. "What place is this?"

"It's Breakstone Hold, the Castle of Duke Venyez in Estile."

"Estile? That's in the Nine."

"It is," the man said. "It is on the Queen's western realms. The bone dragon's name is Visalth, and it's forces seem to be working their way along the alliance. Before Estile, the Duchy of Halnn fell. But the curious thing about the invasion is the pattern of assault. There is no warning, but just before an invasion all magic seems to disappear."

"What?"

"Wizards," the man went on, "witches, mages, even holy paladins seem to disappear. Whether these are physical or spiritual abductions I cannot say. But I do know that when Visalth appears there are none who can stand before him – they all disappear or get destroyed. And now Wendfala is captured, and from her prison she sends me to you ahead of the storm to get your aid."

Kell gulped his tea. The mystical scene vanished but Byrinius still held the glowing ember. My master stood and paced the room. He ran his fingers through his hair again and again. Then he finally stood before the window and gazed out to sea. He stood a long time. He then seemed decisive and strode to a locked wardrobe. He held his fingers over the handle and mumbled a quick verse. The doors popped open and from the inside he drew out a long and stout war-hammer that was glowing brightly.

The weapon was easily as long as my arm. Its handle was wrapped with red leather that showed stains of wear and sweat. The oaken shaft was carved in a hexagon. Cold blue steel ran from the crown down that shaft and was bolted with iron. The broad, flat head could easily have crushed an Ogres Skull, and the opposite side of the hammer was a nasty six sided piece of magical steel ending in a sharp point. The pommel was thick and ended with an 8 inch long double-bladed knife made of Admantium with a magically sharpened blade. Kell tossed his trusty weapon onto the table and the weight of it shook the table and dented it in several places.

"This is my little friend Ashrune," my master said. "How might we help?"

"You need to Flee this place." Byrinius said in a grave and urgent tone.

"Never! I will not run when my Queen's lands are in danger. I am no coward." Kell bellowed, outrage in his voice.

"Bravery in the face of such a monster is suicide," Byrinius said calmly. "The power behind Visalth is cunning, and so you must be just as crafty. Ashrune may be a noble weapon but even with the might of a Titan behind, it would barely scratch the creature's skull before you were impaled. You need something far mightier, and to find such a thing you need help that is beyond simple magic. You need an Angel."

Check out the rest of the story in book or audio book format on my website: www.LordHartRules.com

My Other Books and Audio Books

For A Special Treat, check out my
AUDIO BOOKS

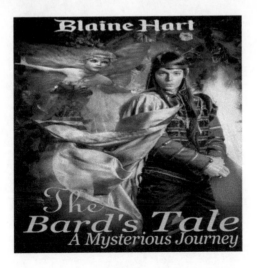

Thanks for reading!

If you enjoyed this book a nice review would be greatly appreciated.

Check Out all My Books and **Audio Books** at:
www.LordHartRules.com